Watersmeet

Also by Nancy Garden

FOURS CROSSING

WATERSMEET

Nancy Garden

Farrar · Straus · Giroux

New York

Copyright © 1983 by Nancy Garden
All rights reserved
Printed in the United States of America
Published simultaneously in Canada by
McGraw-Hill Ryerson Ltd., Toronto
First printing, 1983

Library of Congress catalog card number: 83-11512

*For the Fenn clan,
especially
Aunty and Uncle Dan,
with love*

My thanks to Sandra Scott, for advising me about courtroom procedure. Any errors in legal matters that remain here are mine, not hers.

Watersmeet

1

Thunder shook the mountains surrounding Fours Crossing, New Hampshire. The tiny village rocked and spun, its houses toys in a game played by giants. The rain was like Noah's; the lightning, twisted ropes of snapping fire.

"Warm air meeting cold," said Melissa's father, Stanley Dunn, when at last there was a lull long enough to speak in. He cut himself a second slice of Gran's homemade bread.

Melissa looked questioningly at her grandmother.

"Oh, all right, lambie," Gran said indulgently. A broad smile wrinkled her round weather-beaten face, showing Melissa that her next words weren't to be taken seriously. "Though how anyone can grow up properly without good Scottish porridge for breakfast, I'll never know."

Melissa and her father exchanged a private wink as Melissa pushed her porridge bowl away and reached for the bread knife.

There was a clatter at the back door, and fourteen-year-old Jed Ellison, Melissa's best friend, burst in. Rain streamed from his tattered but taped-together yellow slicker and dripped off the ends of his black hair, where it poked out from under his hood.

"Whew!" Jed shook himself like a wet dog. "I've never seen the like of this," he said in the staccato up-country speech of most Fours Crossing natives. "Seems like all we do is swap one brand of bad weather for another. Snow for all those months and now rain."

Melissa moved Pride and Joy, her grandmother's small black-and-white cat, from the only remaining empty chair at the kitchen table so Jed could sit down.

"I can't stay," Jed said, and then Melissa noticed the worry lines that furrowed his forehead and made his dark, somewhat angular face look older than it was. Jed looked at Gran and then at Melissa's father. "Fact is, I've just come to say that the river's been rising all night, and Mr. Ellison is looking for all the able-bodied men he can find to help shore it up." Henry Ellison, chairman of the Board of Selectmen, which governed the village, was no relation to Jed, even though they had the same last name.

Stanley Dunn sighed. "I suppose," he said, downing the last of his breakfast coffee, "that means me."

"Well," said Jed with a sudden grin, "not necessarily, Mr. Dunn, but . . ."

Stanley flexed his right arm and then his left. "Don't let the gray hair and the semisedentary occupation fool you," he said. "I may be a traveling fund-raiser by trade, but I wouldn't want anyone to forget I'm a Fours Crossing man by birth. And that means able-bodied. Right, Mother?"

"It certainly should," Gran said, a twinkle in her blue-green eyes. Gran's eyes matched Melissa's, but the rest of Melissa, according to Gran anyway, looked like Melissa's mother, who had died the winter before in Boston, where Melissa and her father still officially lived. Melissa had been at Gran's since March, when she had come to visit while her father finished up some business for the fund-raising company he had now left.

Stanley gave Gran a quick hug, kissed Melissa, and squirreled through the careless array of coats and jackets hanging from pegs by the back door.

"Gran?" pleaded Melissa. "Daddy—can I come, too?"

"You're so skinny the wind'll blow you away," Jed teased. "Besides, he said able-bodied *men*."

"Oh, come *on!*" Melissa snapped, as the thunder, now some way off, rolled a defiant and probably only temporary last word. "You're skinnier than I am, Jed Ellison! And I'm just as strong as you even if I am a year younger."

"And no doubt twice as clever as your old dad," said Stanley, tucking a wisp of Melissa's blond hair back into the base of one of her long braids. "But, pigeon, I'll be no good at all if I'm worrying about you. You'd better stay home with Gran."

Gran, however, was already halfway into her boots. "Nonsense," she said. "No one's staying home, except Pride and Joy. Come along, Melissa." Gran handed Melissa a scarf and wrapped one around her own neck—it was May but still chilly—and then plunged her short, square self into a thick pullover before taking her old rubber raincoat from its peg. "Looks as if the worst of the storm's passed for now," she said. "Thank goodness. I'd not have wanted any of us out in that lightning."

The thunder and lightning had indeed subsided, but the rain had not. It came out of the weeping sky in unbroken sheets instead of drops; it streamed under Melissa's collar and scarf and made muddy brooks at both sides of the road that led down from Gran's hilltop house to the river and the village below.

"Frank Grange from the Highway Department says the river's swollen more than he's ever seen it. Dangerous, he called it," Jed shouted as he and Melissa hurried ahead of Gran and

Melissa's father. Jed waited while Melissa skirted an especially deep puddle. "He told me the thaw was so sudden he's not even sure he has enough old feed sacks for sandbags. Farmers are still bringing 'em in, he said."

Melissa shivered involuntarily, remembering what had led to that sudden thaw. When she had come to visit Gran, she had found Fours Crossing frozen, stopped, in what seemed like never-ending winter—and herself thrust into a mystery that even now was only partway solved. Spring, Melissa had learned in school, came each year because of the earth's motion—not, as Jed had insisted, because of an antique silver plate, one of four, that had been stolen from Gran's dining room the summer before. And yet, impossible though it seemed, Melissa now had to admit that Jed had perhaps been right. The snow had started melting not long after she, Jed, and a wonderful half-wild dog named Ulfin had wrested the plate away from the old hermit who'd stolen it, and who had kidnapped Jed and Melissa and held them prisoner for a terrifying two nights.

Melissa shivered again—it was less than a week since they'd been rescued—and carefully waded through another deep puddle. The warm weather had been wonderful at first—sun, blue sky, a few spring birds returning—but with it had come slush from the heaped-up melting snow, and water leaking into houses as layer upon layer of winter ice rapidly melted. At least before the thaw everything was *dry*, Melissa thought ruefully, scrunching her toes away from what she hoped was not a hole in her left boot.

Melissa was just about to ask Jed to stop so she could look at her boot when a small figure, red hair spewing out from under a sodden green wool cap shaped like the top of an acorn, came splashing toward them. "Hi, Tommy," Melissa called, smiling despite the serious expression on her seventh-grade classmate's freckled face. "You look like a duck."

"Quack," Tommy answered promptly. "So do you." Then he turned to Jed. Until recently, Tommy had been known around school as Jed's "shadow," much to Jed's embarrassment. But it had been Tommy who had thought to use Ulfin, now Jed's dog, to find Jed and Melissa when they'd been kidnapped. Ulfin had led Tommy to an old abandoned root cellar deep in the woods, where the hermit had hidden them. No one had called him anyone's shadow since then, Jed least of all.

"They're saying the river'll crest by tonight," Tommy said, falling into step between Jed and Melissa. "Maybe even this afternoon. And if it does . . ."

"If it does," Jed finished, "it'll flood out most of the village. At least everyone who lives around the green."

Tommy nodded. "Mr.-Ellison-the-Selectman's going to evacuate everyone from there," he said importantly. "Maybe even down as far as where we live." Tommy's house was next door to Jed's, across the river from the railroad depot and on the same side as Gran's, but about half a mile away.

"Holy cow!" Jed stopped abruptly and peered over the riverbank.

The brown swirling water, until a few days ago frozen glacier-solid, raced downstream as if trying to get all the way to Boston, two hundred miles south, by nightfall. The water was only about an inch below the level of the bank—which, Melissa realized as Jed pulled her back from it, was already seriously undercut. "It's just a shelf," she said, her mouth suddenly gone dry. "It *bent* when I stepped on it."

"It's sure not going to hold sandbags," said Jed.

"That's why they're putting them a couple of feet back from the edge," said Tommy. "See—over there on the other side. Oh, wow!"

They followed his pointing finger, aimed beyond the knots of people filling sandbags near the railroad depot, and the bucket-brigade line piling the full bags into a stone-wall-like barricade along the riverbank.

"It's that woman again," Jed said in an undertone, his hand making a rain visor over his eyes. "She gives me the creeps."

Melissa could just make out a tall figure, blue against the gray sky, walking slowly toward the sandbag-fillers on the other side of the river—calmly, as if the sun were shining and there was nothing in the world to worry about.

"*I* don't think she's creepy," Tommy said. "I saw her close up yesterday over near Round Top." Round Top was the smallest of the mountains that ringed Fours Crossing, and the one nearest the village. "She was just standing there in the rain, looking off toward Hiltonville."

"Did you speak to her?" Jed asked curiously.

"Not me." Tommy grinned.

Jed shook his head, still watching the woman. "Weird," he said. "I saw her yesterday, too. Not near Round Top, though —in the village. She was buying nails and string and stuff at the general store."

"What's so weird about that?" Melissa asked. She was still too much of a city person to understand the local country-village wariness toward strangers. She watched the woman, who had now joined the others, open and hold a bag while someone else shoveled sand into it. "At least she's helping out."

Tommy turned to Melissa. "Everyone's weird here who's new," he explained. "We even thought *you* were weird at first."

Melissa shot him a wry look. "That's nothing compared to what I thought all of *you* were," she retorted, although it wasn't really true. It had been Jed and Tommy as much as Gran who had made her feel at home in Fours Crossing.

"You thought we were country bumpkins, I bet," said Jed, waving to Gran and Stanley as they passed—but his eyes went quickly back to the woman in blue.

"Come on, you three," Melissa's father called. "If you're going to help, help!" He sounded cheerful, as if in defiance of the obvious danger.

They all crossed the depot bridge. For the next two hours, Jed, Tommy, and Stanley joined the men and women barricading the bank while Melissa shoveled heavy, damp road sand into bags Gran held as firmly as anyone half her age. At last a younger woman took Gran's place, and not long afterward, Melissa, her arms weak and her back too stiff to bend anymore, was able to turn her shovel over to a boy who had just arrived. Then she walked upstream to see how things were in the village. Another bridge, smaller than the one by the depot, spanned the river there, taking the road from Gran's hill into Fours Crossing proper. The river was already swirling against its underside and there was an ominous-looking runnel on the bridge itself, on the village end, where Melissa was.

"Keep back!" Tommy's great-uncle, Mr. Coffin, the postman, called from the other side, where Melissa now noticed a large group of men sandbagging the bank. The few farmhouses below Gran's, she realized, would flood along with the village when the river crested.

As will the bridges, she thought, stunned. How are we going to get back to Gran's if they both wash out before we cross?

But there's no time to think about that! Be sensible, she told herself, knowing that was what her mother would have said.

Melissa had just turned to go back to the sandbag-fillers downstream when tall Mr. Henry Ellison detached himself from the group of men and hurried across to her. "Melissa Dunn," he said, "just the girl we need. Would you pop into the village and tell the folks around the green to get a wiggle-on with their packing? It doesn't look as if we're going to be able to hold this bridge much longer."

Melissa swallowed hard. Mr. Ellison's strong craggy face

was gray and she could see that the men were talking now instead of sandbagging, as if they were trying to think of another, better way to hold the river back. "Where—where should I tell them to go?" she asked.

"Why, bless you!" exclaimed Mr. Ellison, surprise cutting through his well-controlled anxiety. "Don't you know? Your gran's—highest house around." He patted Melissa's shoulder. "That's where we all went in the big flood of '42. After that, she said everyone had a standing invitation. Now go, Melissa, hurry." He glanced at two men unloading what looked like railroad ties from a truck.

So that's why Gran spent all that time yesterday vacuuming a clean house, Melissa thought as she hurried down the rain-slick road—and why she had me buy all those cans of soup even though there's already lots stored down cellar!

The general store was in the first house on the little circular green that marked the center of Fours Crossing. Old Mr. Titus, its owner, and his tiny wife, who was the Town Clerk, were busy loading cartons with bags of flour and rice, cans of coffee and cocoa, flashlights, Band-Aids, wool socks—"Everything," Mrs. Titus said, with surprising cheerfulness given the situation, "we can think of that folks might need. Even," she added, pointing to an orderly row of official-looking wooden boxes along one wall, "the town archives. Can't have them getting all wet and soggy."

Melissa nodded. No one had to tell her how Mrs. Titus felt about the town archives. Weeks earlier, she and Jed had gone to the library to consult a book called *A History of Fours Crossing*, hoping to learn more about the origin of Gran's stolen plate. But just in the place where they were sure the information would be, they found seven pages missing, mysteriously cut out. In the same book they'd discovered that a man named Eli Dunn, the hermit's ancestor and the leader of the village's

10

original settlers, was listed among the people who had died in the year 1725—but without a cause of death beside his name. Since there were explanations for all the other deaths, it seemed to Jed and Melissa almost as if the original Eli Dunn had disappeared instead of dying. That mystery had sent them hurrying to Mrs. Titus for the official town records for 1725. But after confidently going to fetch them, Mrs. Titus, bewilderment deepening the wrinkles in her small face, had reported, "No records at all for that year. None whatsoever at all." Poor Mrs. Titus had been so upset that Melissa could easily understand why she was anxious to protect the remaining archives now, with rain pounding down outside and the river swelling.

"Where's that kerosene, Mother?" asked Mr. Titus, peering at his wife over the tops of his spectacles. His small, sharp face, puckered with worry, showed that he took the situation much more seriously than Mrs. Titus, who seemed to view it more as an adventure than an impending disaster.

"Top shelf—no, t'other one," Mrs. Titus answered as Melissa hurried out to the post office. "Thank you, dear," Mrs. Titus called after her. "We're just about ready now, anyway."

Empty mail bags bulged heavily over the edges of the post office's top shelves; two half-full ones lay in a lumpy heap on the floor. "Today's incoming and outgoing," explained the postmistress, Mrs. Dupres, wife of the police chief, indicating the bags with uneasy little flutters of her hand. "D'you suppose I could take the incoming up to your grandmother's, Melissa?" she asked. "Give folks something to read, anyway."

Melissa nodded.

"As to the outgoing," Mrs. Dupres went on as if to herself, "well, I s'pose I'd best take that, too, hadn't I? It's sure not to go out till all this is over, and it wouldn't do to turn it into papier-mâché." She giggled nervously.

Melissa ran on around the green, knocking on doors and

rousing people, though few really needed rousing, only hurrying. Everyone, she realized, from Mrs.-Ellison-the-librarian to Mrs.-Ellison-in-the-school-office (neither of whom was directly related to Jed, either) had been packing for hours. Every motorized vehicle in the village, including the fire truck and the police cruiser, was already overflowing with cartons and suitcases and lined up as if for a race under the watchful bronze eyes of the statue that rose wetly but serenely from the center of the green. The statue was of Bradford Ellison, first minister in Fours Crossing; he *was* a relative—an ancestor—of Jed's, though a distant one.

By the time Melissa got back to the river, a fresh, strong wind had come up, and renewed thunder rumbled ominously in the distance. She arrived just as tall Mr.-Ellison-the-Selectman straightened up from inspecting the underside of the village bridge. "Looks like it's time, Zeb," Melissa heard him say gravely to Mr. Coffin. "Best go tell Pete to sound the alarm."

Melissa, swallowing panic, turned downstream to find her father and grandmother but was stopped by the first of the cars already beginning to roll out of the village. Police Chief Dupres, a large, reassuringly sturdy man who took his job— usually—with a dash of humor, had stationed himself at the threatened bridge, directing cars across, slowly, one at a time. A raincoat-clad arm waved wildly at Melissa from an old Ford that bulged with schoolbooks, artwork, rolled-up maps and papers, and a familiar face—her teacher, Miss Laurent's— leaned out and called, "Melissa!" followed by what might have been "Want a ride?" Melissa shook her head, realizing the wind was too strong for Miss Laurent to hear her answer— and then the fire siren shrieked its warning over another, closer clap of thunder.

2

Melissa felt as if she were the last human being on earth as she struggled downstream toward the depot bridge, as close to the furiously racing river as she dared. Branches sped by, tangled with fenceposts and pieces of lumber that looked as if they might have come at least from woodsheds if not from houses. There was even a small, incongruously bright-red rocking chair spinning dizzily along in its own whirlpool. "Daddy!" Melissa tried to shout; "Jed! Tommy! Gran"—but it was no use. The wind snatched her words and took them away as fast as it took the river. If, Melissa told herself as she approached the depot, trying to be sensible, I don't find them and both bridges go, I'll just veer off at right angles to the river. The land's got to go up, with all these mountains. She peered to her right as she ran, looking for the steepest slope. But that was no use, either; the falling rain made an impenetrable curtain.

She found Jed at last, by nearly running into him. He gripped her arm, mouthed "Don't move," and disappeared into the gloom, returning in a moment with Melissa's father, who immediately put a strong arm around each of them.

"Gran?" Melissa shouted, a thin bleat in the wind.

"Okay—house," her father shouted back, thin too.

Melissa wanted to ask about Tommy, but the storm blew her question away. Wind whipped their clothes and tore Melissa's hair out of its braids as the three of them made a human chain and began to struggle back upstream.

"No! Dog!" Jed shouted, breaking out of the chain. "Got—to—get—Ulfin—at home!" He staggered back toward the depot bridge before they could stop him, disappearing almost instantly behind the gray curtain of rain.

Melissa's father cupped his hand over Melissa's ear and said "Belt," motioning her to take hers off her raincoat as he removed his own. Then he buckled the two belts together and tied Melissa to him, pulling her along after Jed with his weight as well as his strength.

Just as they reached the depot bridge, Ulfin, strong legs braced against the wind and silky gold coat wildly rippling, led Jed across to them. Ulfin nudged Melissa in greeting, and when she leaned awkwardly down to pat him, he licked her face gently, making it as wet with his soft tongue as it already was from the rain, but calming her.

"My dad," Jed shouted, waving a limp piece of paper—a note, Melissa guessed, from its size and the words rivering bluely down it. "Says—near—village—bridge. Waiting—for us—truck. Dad's—helping—clear out—village."

Stanley Dunn nodded and linked arms with Jed; Ulfin, now leashed, pressed tightly against Jed's outer leg. They went on, following the raging river, pushing themselves into the wind, till at last they heard a rumble that wasn't thunder and saw the glow of headlights from Seth Ellison's battered red-and-white pickup truck. Jed's dad, who looked like an older, somewhat moodier version of Jed, leaned out and pulled them in one at a time. The heater, Melissa realized gratefully as she squeezed between Jed and her father, with Ulfin more or less on everyone's laps, was on full.

"Where'n tarnation were you?" Seth asked Jed. "I've made three trips—well, never mind. But I'd almost given you up and gone back for Ulfin." Seth, obviously relieved to see his son, eased the truck carefully into first gear and crept cautiously onto the bridge, which, Melissa saw to her horror, was now awash with water—how deep, she couldn't tell. "Another few minutes and . . . Just keep an eye out there, Stanley, would you?" Seth said to Melissa's father. "Want to make sure I've got 'er nice and square-like on the high part if I can."

Melissa's father rolled down his window. "You're fine, Seth, fine . . ." Suddenly Melissa felt her father's body stiffen; his head turned sharply to look over his shoulder behind them. "Gun it, Seth," he said calmly, but with such force that Seth immediately slammed his accelerator to the floor.

Melissa heard a gurgle and then a rushing sound, like a waterfall. With growing dread, she turned to look out the back window—and there, coming over the bridge, covering where they'd been as soon as they left it, was the river, chasing them to high ground.

Cars and trucks lined the hill road and the driveway leading to Gran's; inside, the house was jumbled chaos. To get from one room to another, especially downstairs, one had to climb over outstretched feet and legs, and weave through a forest of hands holding soup plates, stew bowls, sandwiches, mugs of cocoa or coffee, and glasses of whiskey, the latter being freely dispensed by Frank Grange of the Highway Department. Mrs. Dupres, looking much calmer now, followed him with the incoming mail.

"No, thank you, Frank," Seth Ellison said evenly as Melissa, Jed, and their two fathers dripped their exhausted way through the front hall. "I'm still on the wagon." Melissa caught Jed's shy smile at his father; Seth Ellison had become an alcoholic after his wife's death some years back and had eventually lost both his carpentry job and his son's respect because of it. But Jed's being kidnapped by the hermit had shaken him out of that, at least so far. Seth had helped Tommy, Ulfin, and Melissa's father hunt for Jed and Melissa, and ever since they'd found them, Seth hadn't touched anything stronger than Gran's good country coffee—which she now came through the hall pouring generously from a huge pot Melissa hadn't seen before.

"*There* you are." Gran beamed at them, as serene as if she were serving at a church social. "Best you get out of those wet clothes—Jed, Seth, I'm sure Stanley's got something you can borrow." She chuckled. "I daresay you didn't have time to pack."

"Got a couple of suitcases in the truck, Miz Dunn, but thanks," Seth said, accepting a mug of coffee. Melissa and Gran exchanged a wink; Seth had suddenly become almost vain about his appearance, now that he'd stopped drinking. "Figured Stanley wouldn't have clothes to spare," he explained, "just being in town for a visit and all."

"Oh, I don't know," said Stanley Dunn, glancing out the window. "I have a feeling this visit's going to last so long Fours Crossing's going to feel like home again."

Smiling, Melissa went upstairs, where she found plump Joan Savage, who sat next to her in school, and four other girls from her class camped out in her small blue-and-white room above the dining room. She greeted them quickly and changed into dry jeans and her favorite dark-red turtleneck before hurrying back downstairs to see if Gran needed help in the kitchen. It was fun, having a houseful—like having an enormous family—except, she thought, stepping around

16

people perched on the stairs as she went back down—except I wish I'd been here long enough to learn all their names . . .

"Hi there, Melissa!" That was someone she knew—Chief Dupres's lanky, often outspoken sergeant, Charley, who had helped Chief Dupres arrest the hermit and take him to jail in Hiltonville, a little over ten miles away. "If you manage to get through to the kitchen, I'd sure take a liking to another of your gran's Toll House cookies."

A chorus of agreement went up from the cluster of police, fire, and Highway Department men around Charley, and for the next half hour or so, Melissa was kept busy passing cookies and taking orders for sandwiches, which were being made assembly-line fashion by a team of women in Gran's busy kitchen. Jed was trotting up and down the cellar stairs with armloads of wood for Gran's three fireplaces: the huge one in the kitchen, on whose hearth Pride and Joy and Ulfin snoozed warily in opposite corners, and the smaller back-to-back ones in the dining and living rooms. Melissa's father, Gran told Melissa as she went back to get a third refill for the cookie plate, had gone out again to help lead the animals from the riverside farms to safety higher up the hill. There were already several strange chickens in the henhouse, Gran went on to say, and she'd appreciate it if Melissa would look in as soon as she could and make sure the barriers improvised by their owners were holding and no one was pecking anyone else. "And Tommy's cousin, little Susie Coffin," Gran added, heaping cookies, "found a half-drowned rabbit in her front yard and wanted to know if she could put it in your room. I said down cellar, but in the storeroom, away from people's dogs and cats. Oh, and Tommy Coffin's mother wants to know if you've seen him."

"I haven't," Melissa said. "I'll look."

But at that point the electricity went off, and the women

in the kitchen quickly lit the kerosene lamps Gran had placed in readiness. Soon warm light from the lamps and from the kitchen fire made dancing stars on the copper bottoms of Gran's hanging pots and sent shadows leaping to the herbs and onions that hung in bunches from the kitchen beams.

As Melissa left the room, Gran was calmly transferring stew from a pot on the now-dead electric stove to a large iron kettle suspended on a crane in the fireplace, and Miss Laurent was starting a song. No one seemed very worried about either the storm or Tommy, but Melissa, realizing she hadn't seen him since before she'd helped fill sandbags, went from room to room looking for him. Everyone was singing now: the food crew seated tiredly around Gran's kitchen table; the elderly people on comfortable chairs and cushions near the fire in the living room; the policemen, firemen, Highway Department men, and various town officials in the hall; schoolchildren (no Tommy among them) perched on the stairs—everyone except one or two sixth-graders—who were on duty in the cellar supervising the dogs and cats, and the toddlers and babies, who were tucked away upstairs, supposedly napping. All the remaining adults were in the dining room, where Gran's four antique silver plates, proudly reunited, hung in a circle on one whitewashed wall, and her collection of tiles, trivets, and antique silver spoons blinked cheerfully at a multicolored tapestry that hung on another. Thunder crashed outside again and jagged lightning ropes lashed the sky, but everyone was safe and warm and dry—except maybe Tommy, Melissa thought, worried now, going up to her father when he came back into the kitchen from helping with the farm animals.

Just as she was about to ask him if he'd seen Tommy, there was an excited murmur from the front hall. Melissa ran out in time to see Tommy's father, his raincoat glistening in the light from the kerosene barn lantern he held, shaking his head and gesturing toward the front door. Then Miss Laurent's clear voice rose above the others, saying, "Why don't we take a roll call, house by house? We know who's supposed to be here, but it's so crowded it's hard to keep track. Someone get the kids from upstairs."

Small pajamaed and blanketed figures sleepily joined larger, more conventionally dressed ones on the stairs, and families sounded off one by one according to their names and where they lived—the Tituses, the Savages; the Laurents and La-Bontes and Nickersons; the Dupreses and the Granges and the Goodels; the Hendersons and Campbells and MacAllisters and Williamses; the Bartholomés and Evanses and Duponts; the many different Ellison families and the several Coffins . . .

The Coffins—all accounted for but Tommy.

3

It was only at Gran's insistence that Melissa tried to sleep—
Jed, too, she realized when she saw Gran sternly coming
upstairs several steps behind him. Jed tiptoed reluctantly past
the hall storage chest on which Melissa was more or less
bedded down with an old mothball-smelling quilt. "Any
news?" she whispered, stopping him.

He shook his head. "I wish they'd let me help look," he
grumbled, sitting down on the edge of the chest. "Ulfin would
find him—if he's to be found," he added darkly. "I'm just glad
I know the hermit's safe in jail."

"Of course he's safe in jail," Gran said, reaching the hall,
puffing a little. "And of course Tommy will be found. Back
to the spare room with the other boys now, laddie—scoot."

"Yes, Miz Dunn," he said gloomily, and trailed off, leaving
Melissa to lie there, eyes wide open in the dark, listening fruit-
lessly for the clatter and excitement that she knew would ac-
company Tommy's being found.

But it never came.

As soon as it was light and she heard people stirring, Melissa
got up and went down to the kitchen, where she found

Tommy's mother, barely under control, pouring coffee for his father and great-uncle. Melissa's own father and Jed's were at the table, too, silent and drawn after helping hunt for Tommy all night. Jed came in just as Melissa was about to go looking for him, and after a hastily thrown-together breakfast, they put on their still-damp raincoats, called quietly to Ulfin, and set off down the hill.

The rain had stopped, though the sky was thick with clouds and the sun could do no more than make one section a bit brighter than the rest. Water dripped from branches so steadily that after a minute Melissa thought the rain had started again till she looked up—and then, awe momentarily driving her worry away, she cried "Look!" to Jed. Above her was the first hint of green—tiny damp beginnings of leaves peeping out from opening buds. "Spring!" both she and Jed said simultaneously, and then laughed. But they soon stopped, remembering Tommy—and sobered by the sight that greeted them at the bottom of the hill.

The river had widened into a lake, quiet at the edges but with a quickly running current in the center. There was no sign of either bridge. Brown water lapped the porch of a house to their left, staining its white paint; a few yards beyond, it lapped the bottoms of first-floor windows. They couldn't get close enough to the village to see how high the water was there, but Melissa imagined that the Bradford Ellison statue must be at least up to its shoulders, looking sadly out at rooftops instead of at whole houses.

Downstream from the village, on Gran's side of the river, Tommy's house and Jed's next door were like islands in a pond. Nearly two feet of water stood in the Coffins' living room. Jed managed to slog through it in his high boots and go upstairs to Tommy's room, where he got a sock for Ulfin to sniff.

"Find Tommy, Ulfin," he said, when they were outside again; he knelt and looked into the dog's gold-brown eyes, flecked with color. Ulfin looked back steadily, unlike most dogs, and Melissa remembered how when he'd first met her own eyes that way, she'd been unable to move.

"Find Tommy, Ulfin," Jed said again.

Ulfin gave the sock a polite sniff, then took it delicately in his teeth and dropped it to the ground at Jed's feet, as if he had no need of it. Without hesitation, he turned and ran upstream along the riverbank.

Jed and Melissa followed Ulfin past the village, close enough to it so that Melissa could see even from across the river that it was not flooded to the rooftops after all but only to the middles of people's first-floor windows. They went on past the boggy fields on the village's outskirts, and up into the high rolling meadow country that Melissa could not remember seeing without a heavy covering of snow.

"Where's Ulfin going?" she asked as she struggled to keep up with Jed. He was almost running himself.

"Beats me," Jed answered. "But *he* sure seems to know."

It was true. Ulfin was running as surely as any bloodhound —but with his nose up, apparently not needing a scent. Melissa felt much more optimistic about Tommy when she saw that.

At the base of a large oak tree, Ulfin wheeled at right angles to the river and ran toward the hills Melissa could see rising to mountains in the distance. The sun broke through suddenly, making water drops look like crystal baubles on the tips of branches. The ground was still spongy underfoot, but in the new gold light Melissa could see green shoots thrusting up through the thatched brown grass. She wanted to shout to Ulfin to stop so she could savor the sight, but he was too far ahead and running too fast.

22

"Round Top," Jed panted, trying to strip off his slicker as he ran. "He's headed up Round Top Mountain."

The ground began to steam under the steadily warming sun, and Melissa, struggling out of her coat, too, wished she hadn't put her thick red sweater on over her turtleneck that morning—but even though most of the snow had already melted or washed away, the temperature still hadn't risen much above 40 or so. It feels like at least 80 now, she thought, as Ulfin led them steadily up what appeared to be a faint path, rough and rocky but wide.

"It's an old fire road," Jed explained, panting. "Practically no one comes up here anymore, except hikers in the summer. Your gran told me once that people used to graze sheep here, way back in the old days. Couple of tumbledown shacks and sheep pens is all that's left of that now. Ulfin, wait up!" he called ahead.

But Ulfin only turned his head and barked them on—as if he's more eager than worried, Melissa thought, scrambling over rocks and occasional snow patches—he almost seems to be looking forward to something.

About halfway up Round Top, Melissa saw a bright-blue sparkle below them. A lake, she thought, till she pointed it out to Jed and he, pausing a moment to look, said, "The village. That's the floodwater shining. Looks harmless from here, doesn't it? But think of all those wet rugs and books and shorted-out stoves and refrigerators and things."

Another impatient bark from Ulfin urged them forward, and they plodded ahead, too tired to go on running. The fire road grew rapidly both steeper and narrower, till it ended in a single barely discernible track. "We're not far from the top now," said Jed, wiping the sweat off his forehead. "Only thing is, I can't figure out what Tommy could be doing up here, unless he panicked at the water last night and ran . . ."

"Listen," said Melissa.

A faint, sweetly sad music came to them as the light wind shifted—soft singing accompanied by muted but clear liquid notes. Ulfin stopped and stood trembling—not with fear, Melissa realized, watching him closely—more with joy.

"No barks?" said Jed softly, watching Ulfin also and then frowning as the music came closer and he still didn't move.

Around a bend in what was left of the path ahead appeared the same tall young woman Tommy had pointed out to them at the river the day before. She was wearing a light-blue cloak-like garment with the hood thrown back, and had a small harp nestled in the crook of her arm.

Ulfin's ears went forward and twitched, but he was motionless, except for his gently waving tail.

"A fine day for walking," said the woman cheerfully, nodding toward Ulfin and holding out her free hand for him to sniff. "But it is Tommy Coffin, not the sun, that brings you here, I'll warrant."

"Um—er—yes," stammered Jed.

Melissa found herself unable to take her eyes off the woman. There was something hauntingly beautiful about her whole manner as well as her appearance. Her quiet blue eyes matched the shimmering water below and gave an air of deep serenity to her pale, reservedly friendly face. Thick black hair fell over her shoulders in a shining ebony cascade, and the graceful hand that she now worked around to the back of Ulfin's neck, stroking, moved with a sure and gentle strength that Ulfin clearly found irresistible.

"Your friend Tommy is fine now, well and dry," the woman said, smiling directly at Melissa. "It was because he fell into the river that I kept him with me last night. I hope his people will understand. It was not possible to send word."

24

"You kept him *here*?" sputtered Jed. "On Round Top? But there's no place . . ."

"Come," said the woman, still smiling. "I will take you to him." She turned and walked away from them, beckoning them to follow.

"I don't like this," Jed muttered. "No one knows who she is or—or anything. And she talks funny—old-fashioned, sort of."

"Ulfin likes her," Melissa pointed out, feeling perfectly at ease with the woman herself—and sure enough, Ulfin, tail still gently wagging, was walking slowly beside the woman; her hand was resting lightly on his head.

"Ulfin!" Jed called sharply.

But all Ulfin did was look around and give his tail a couple of extra, faster wags, as if to reassure Jed.

After about a hundred yards, the woman turned into thick underbrush at one side of the path. Melissa heard the sound of water as they followed, and soon they came through the brush to a rapid, stony brook, not far from which was a small stone cottage chinked with moss, rather like the picture of a Scottish crofter's cottage that hung in Gran's front hall.

"Tommy," the woman called. "Tommy!"

"She just ate," came Tommy's voice from inside the cottage —calm, everyday, as if nothing had happened. "Just a little milk. And Linnet's been licking her . . . oh!"

Tommy, rumpled but dry, his acorn cap half in, half out of his hip pocket, appeared at the low door, a blanket-wrapped bundle in his arms. "Hi, Jed," he said, blinking in the sunlight. "Melissa. Gee, you didn't have to come all this way! Hi, Ulfin." He reached out to pat the dog, who was sniffing eagerly around the door, wagging his tail harder.

"He smells Linnet," said Tommy, smiling at the woman, while Melissa and Jed still stared. It's as if he were in his own front yard, Melissa thought in amazement; as if there'd been no flood and he came up here every afternoon.

"Might I be introduced?" asked the woman, and Tommy, suddenly red-faced, pointed to them each in turn with his blanketed bundle. "Sorry. This is Melissa Dunn—and this is Jed Ellison—and this . . ." He reddened still more. "You better say it," he said to the woman. "I'm not sure I'd get it right."

"Jed, Melissa," said the woman, with little formal nods toward each of them, "welcome. I have many names, but the one your friend knows is Rhiannon."

The name echoed the sound of the brook where it ran smoothly over polished pebbles. Melissa wasn't surprised that Tommy had trouble saying it.

Rhiannon bent over the bundle in Tommy's arms. "This is the reason your friend fell into the river," she said, folding back a corner of the blanket.

Melissa moved closer and looked down into the remote but intelligent, black-barred amber eyes of the tiniest goat she had ever seen.

"She's still a kid," Tommy said. "A baby doe—that means female, like with deer. Probably only a few weeks old, Rhian—non says. I got mixed up yesterday in the storm," he explained, "after the sandbagging. I thought I was heading for my house, but I'd already passed it, I think, and then I heard this crying and—well, there she was in the river, this little goat. So I pulled her out . . ."

"You pulled her *out?*" said Jed incredulously. "Of the *river* when it was flooding?"

Tommy blushed again, but looked pleased at Jed's obvious admiration. "It had calmed down some," he said modestly. "You'd have done the same." He stroked the little goat between her sturdy ears. "Anyway, I—well, I was still sort of lost and going the wrong way and all. Rhiannon found me partway up here." He gestured toward the goat with his chin. "Isn't she neat?"

"Oh, yes!" exclaimed Melissa. "May I hold her?" She looked up at Rhiannon.

Rhiannon's blue eyes smiled down into hers, and Melissa felt unaccountably warmed by them and very safe. "If she will let you," Rhiannon said. "Take her over to the sun and let her feel its warmth on her. She still needs comforting."

Melissa carefully took the goat from Tommy, carried her to an especially sunny spot near the brook, and, after putting her gently on the ground, loosened the blanket. The goat lay there for a second, looking around, ears and nose twitching with curiosity. Then she bounded sturdily to her feet, nuzzling Melissa and wagging her stubby gray tail. "Look, Jed," Melissa cried in delight, "look, she . . ."

"Careful," said Jed suddenly as Ulfin left off sniffing the door and came over to Melissa, tail straight out instead of wagging. "Dogs and goats don't . . ."

"These will, I think," Rhiannon said quietly, and Ulfin touched the goat's nose with his and then walked away, to Rhiannon this time. He sat in front of her, holding out his paw as he had when he'd first met Melissa, in the snow by Gran's mailbox.

"Ulfin's Jed's dog now," Tommy explained to Rhiannon when she took Ulfin's paw in her hand. "But he started out as a sort of a stray. He just kind of showed up in Fours Crossing at about the same time Melissa did, and if it hadn't been for him, Melissa and Jed might still be up in the woods with the hermit—that's this old guy who's some kind of distant relative of Melissa's, and he's the Forest Keeper, or was, which is an old job that doesn't matter much anymore, except at . . ."

But Tommy's eager voice trailed off; Rhiannon didn't seem

to be paying attention. Instead, she was stroking Ulfin and examining the gold tag that hung from his three-stranded gold collar. The tag spelled out his name in regular letters on one side. But on the other his name was engraved in the same mysterious cipher that spelled out SPRINGE, SOMMER, FALL, WYNTER on the four plates that hung in Gran's dining room; the SPRINGE plate was the one the hermit had stolen. The cipher letters also matched those in an old diary Jed and Melissa had found in the hermit's—the Forest Keeper's— house deep in the woods behind Gran's. Melissa still had some of its pages, for the diary's binding had come apart while she held it, and she had spent many hours matching the thin spidery cipher symbols written on them to letters of the real alphabet.

"We'd better go," Jed was saying nervously—but there was a sudden commotion by the cottage door. Melissa turned and saw what looked like a smaller, younger version of Ulfin frisk out, her high-pitched barking punctuated by merry circular wags of a high plumed tail.

"Ulfin!" Jed called warningly as Ulfin stood up.

"It will be all right," Rhiannon said quietly. "Here, Linnet." Immediately the half-grown pale-gold puppy stopped barking and stood quietly beside her mistress while Ulfin, with a mixture of eagerness and dignity, sniffed her carefully. Then he stood still while Linnet, released by a nod from Rhiannon, squiggled around him, belly to the ground, sniffing also but not quite touching him, as if out of respect for his greater age. A moment later, though, politeness worn off, she took Ulfin's tail playfully in her mouth and shook it, worrying it like a stick.

They all laughed, even Jed, and Ulfin looked amused, turning his head to watch. Linnet sat down, her eyes merry, Ulfin's tail still in her mouth.

"Well met," said Rhiannon, holding out her hands to Jed and Melissa. "Come, let me give you some tea before you take Tommy home." She picked up the young doe gently and put her in a pen by the door. "Dogs, guard her well," she said, and then led Melissa, Jed, and Tommy inside.

4

The cottage was low-ceilinged, dark, and a little musty; no one, it appeared, had lived there for a long time. A broom in one corner along with a water-filled bucket with a rag draped over it showed someone had been cleaning, as did the fresh straw strewn on the floor under the single low glassless window. Another rag was draped over the end of a large battered floor loom, as if someone had been dusting. Rhiannon explained she had found the loom in the cottage; Melissa could see that it was already partly dressed with a warp of fine but strong-looking blue and brown wool, the blue incongruously bright against the dark, deeply scarred wood. A pile of smoky-gray kittens lay curled up together on a narrow, hard-looking cot at one side of the small fireplace. Four rough wooden chairs around a rougher table, plus several cupboards whose doors hung open, completed the furnishings—no faucets for running water, as far as Melissa could see, no electric lights, no refrigerator.

But Rhiannon, without apologies, poured water from a brown-and-tan crockery pitcher into a kettle suspended in the fireplace and blew glowing ashes into flames.

"Storm waifs," she said, nodding toward the kittens, whom Melissa was watching longingly.

"Like me," Tommy laughed, adjusting the position of his acorn cap in his pocket and sitting down. "And like all the ones outside. You should see what she's got. A raccoon and two rabbits and this neat baby porcupine and a little sparrow hawk with a hurt wing and a couple of foxes and about four hundred mice and a toad and—what is it, three squirrels?"

"Four," said Rhiannon, setting out loose tea and a brown pot. "I have no milk and no sugar, but the tea is made from herbs and very tasty, so you may not miss them. No lemon, either," she added, apparently as an afterthought.

"My grandmother sometimes makes herb tea," said Melissa, anxious to please, nudging Jed under the table with her foot.

"Right," said Jed quickly. "We're—er—used to it."

"Good," said Rhiannon, smiling. She put a wooden plate of flat biscuits—scones—on the table. "No butter, I am afraid. And no jam. I made these scones the old way, on the open fire, but now that I have cleaned away the oven's soot, I shall have to try baking them, as many people do today." She pointed to a small oblong opening at one side of the fireplace, like Gran's fireplace oven, Melissa thought, but not as fancy. And certainly not modern, as Rhiannon seemed to think.

"How long have you lived here?" Jed asked curiously after they had chatted for a while, waiting for the kettle to boil. "You're not—well, you're not *from* around here, are you?"

"No," Rhiannon answered. "I came when the rain did," she said, passing scones.

"But . . ." began Jed.

"And," interrupted Tommy, as always eager to be the bearer of news, "she found this little house empty and it was pouring rain, so she moved in and found lots of mice and things living here—and—and then the flood came and then me and the goat . . ."

Rhiannon took the kettle off the fire and, after rinsing the pot out with hot water as Gran did, added tea, and then poured in more water. "There," she said, setting the pot on the table. "It should steep a few minutes—you must have a great thirst after your climb."

Melissa nodded politely; she was thirsty, but for something cold; she'd never understood how people could think of hot tea as a remedy for thirst. Gran did sometimes, though, and people often did in English books. That's it, she realized, glancing suddenly at Rhiannon, that's what she talks like besides old-fashioned—not quite English, exactly, but not American, either, with a musical lift at the ends of sentences that ought to make them questions but doesn't quite.

But it seemed rude to ask her straight out where she was from.

Rhiannon fetched cups from one of the open cupboards—none of them matched or had saucers—and poured a drop of tea into one. "Not quite ready," she said.

"Are you—are you going to live here?" asked Jed, shifting a bit nervously in his chair. "I mean," he added, "it'll be okay in warm weather, I guess, but come winter . . ."

"Oh," said Rhiannon, gazing out the window, "I hope I will no longer be needed by winter."

Melissa and Jed exchanged glances.

"Needed?" asked Tommy.

"Yes," Rhiannon said, turning back to them with her enigmatic smile and at last pouring the tea. "I have come because of a relative."

"Oh," said Jed, openly relieved. "Who? Fours Crossing is so little," he explained, "everyone knows just about everyone else." He grinned. "I bet your relative is named Ellison. Fours

Crossing is so full of Ellisons that it's probably the only town in the whole country where there are more E's than S's in the phone book."

But Rhiannon only smiled again and said, "My relative is not an Ellison." She raised her cup to her lips and looked at them over the rim. "But perhaps you can tell me how I might get to where he is—Hiltonville, I believe it is called. I must go there very soon."

Jed looked a little as if he wanted to say, "The same way you got here," but Melissa gave him a sharper nudge under the table and he kept quiet. Tommy said, "Oh, almost anybody could take you. Someone's always going there to shop or see doctors and stuff. And all the older kids go to high school there." He glanced at Jed. "It's really not that far away. And now that it's spring—hey, Melissa, maybe you could go up there now that the snow's melted."

Melissa smiled at Rhiannon. "I'm new here, too," she explained. "Although not quite so new as you."

Rhiannon put her hand over Melissa's for a moment and squeezed it. "I know," she said softly. Then she quickly passed the scones again.

Melissa took one but didn't eat it, and for a moment she turned away, not understanding why it should be that tears had leapt to her eyes at Rhiannon's touch. But later, when Rhiannon showed them the animals in their improvised cages in a sheep pen out back, Melissa understood: Rhiannon's hands, whenever she touched another living creature, were so like Melissa's mother's that Melissa had to turn away.

"Well, I think she's terrific," Tommy insisted as they scrambled quickly back down Round Top, feeling guilty because of Tommy's worried parents.

"Me too," said Melissa. "What's the matter with you, Jed?

You seemed to like her after a while. Now you don't again. Just give me one good reason for *not* liking her—go on."

"He can't," said Tommy. "Suspicious old mountain man! You're as bad as Mr. Titus in the store," he teased. Then he turned to Melissa. "I'll bet a lot of people in the village will think she's weird just because she's not living in a regular house. And because no one knows her. That's it, Jed, isn't it? But it's dumb."

Jed picked up a stone from the side of the fire road and tossed it into the woods. Ulfin looked at him quizzically, but Jed ignored him, and Ulfin walked on. "It's partly those things," Jed said slowly. "Well, I guess it mostly is. But it's also not knowing how she got here. I mean, there's no car or anything. Of course, maybe someone gave her a ride, but still, why come here in the middle of the rain? Why not wait till good weather? And she talks so funny . . ."

"She told us she was here because of a relative in Hiltonville," Melissa said defensively. "I suppose she'd have had to come rain or no rain if she was going to visit someone."

"Well, why not stay with them, then?" Jed retorted. "Or at least in Hiltonville if they don't have room. There are hotels there and restaurants and everything. Why stay in an old tumbledown shack practically on top of a mountain?"

Tommy shrugged. "Maybe she likes camping out. And maybe her ride only came as far as here."

"Did you see the way she looked at Ulfin's collar?" Jed asked Melissa, ignoring Tommy, who turned away as if his feelings were hurt.

Melissa nodded uncomfortably; that had puzzled her, too. Most people would have asked what the cipher letters meant. But Rhiannon hadn't . . .

"As if," said Jed, completing her unspoken thought, "she could read it."

"Well," Melissa said stubbornly, shaking off her uncomfortable feeling, "it's not all that hard a cipher. I mean, *we* solved it, so it can't be all that hard. And even . . ."

"The hermit," Jed reminded her, interrupting, "is in jail in Hiltonville."

Gran's side of the riverbank, when they came down off Round Top, was seething with activity. Two search parties, one led by Chief Dupres and the other by his sergeant, Charley, were comparing notes at the temporary ferry landing that had been set up where the village bridge used to be. They stopped talking as soon as Melissa, Jed, and Tommy came into view, and stared at Tommy as if he were a ghost. Then Tommy's father burst out of the group of men and ran toward them, shouting with joy, and Tommy, looking very embarrassed, allowed himself to be hugged and thumped on the back and made much of before being taken home to his worried mother. The people swarming along the riverbanks looked up from their staggering loads of mud-covered furniture, soggy books, and filthy, shapeless curtains and rugs to greet Tommy as Jed, Melissa, and the search parties escorted him home. Joan Savage, capably rowing her mother and one other woman across the river, tossed her dark hair in an awkward hello and shouted, "Hey, Tommy! Glad you're back!" Behind the Savages' boat was a makeshift raft loaded with suitcases, blankets, and an enormous puffy red quilt.

Melissa and Jed left Tommy to be fussed over by Mrs. Coffin and went next door to Jed's house. The water had already begun to recede, so they helped Seth carry every stick of furniture, every picture, every cushion, out to the back yard to dry. "I've never seen so much mud!" Melissa exclaimed, scraping layers of it off plates in the kitchen, and Jed, tossing limp boxes of cereal and other spoiled food into a trash can

35

for the dump, said, "You'd see a lot more if you looked in a mirror!"

That night Gran's house was full again, for most people's homes were still too wet for them to move back. The regular twice-a-week freight train made an unscheduled stop in Fours Crossing to deliver bottled drinking water from downstate, and the next morning a truck took samples from Fours Crossing wells to the state capital to check for contamination. School was put off indefinitely, partly so the old frame house that was its building could dry out and so Mrs.-Ellison-in-the-school-office could try to reconstruct some badly water-damaged records—but also so the children could help clean up the village.

Before the second day ended, most families had done just about all they could for their own belongings. Mr. Henry Ellison tacked sign-up sheets to the bulletin boards in the general store and post office so people could volunteer for public cleanup jobs. Melissa and Jed, after crossing the river in the Savages' boat, which had officially been put into service as the town ferry, both put their names down under LIBRARY. The name Rhiannon, with an illegible last name after it, was at the end of two longish columns, GENERAL STORE and POST OFFICE.

"I never expected the water to go so high," sighed Fours Crossing's elderly but energetic librarian—another Mrs. Ellison—when Melissa and Jed reported for duty Thursday morning. "I emptied only the bottom shelf before the flood."

All that morning Melissa and Jed carried soggy, waterlogged books outside to the rapidly drying lawn behind the church, whose basement housed the library, and spread them to dry in the sun. "Don't try opening the books yet," Mrs. Ellison cautioned, coming out with several mud-stained card-catalog drawers in her arms.

Melissa, carrying an armful of books, several from the shelf that had once been marked TOWN HISTORY, nodded. She'd just tried to open *A History of Fours Crossing*, the book in which she and Jed had looked up the hermit's ancestor not long before. But it was stuck together almost as firmly as if it had been glued, despite the small gap left by the seven missing pages.

Mrs. Ellison set the card-catalog trays down heavily. "There!" she said, pushing a wisp of white hair off her forehead. "*T* through Z. I wish I dared pull the pins out and dump out the cards—but I'm afraid they'll blow away. As to the books," she said, with a sigh, looking around, "well, once the phones work again I'll call the main library in the capital and try to find out more about how to save wet books. I think I read somewhere about freezing them or refrigerating them or something like that." She fingered the spine of one old book lovingly and Melissa realized she was fighting tears. But Mrs. Ellison soon rallied, dabbing at her eyes with a tattered tissue. "For now," she said, smiling at Jed and Melissa bravely, "all I can think of is spreading the books out in the sun. I'm just so afraid that's the wrong thing—but if they don't dry soon, they'll get covered with mildew, I'm sure."

"I bet we can at least open the ones that didn't get soaked through," Melissa said, trying to cheer her up. She experimented with balancing some of the drier books on their covers so they made little tents with their pages hanging down. "Look," she said, "the air can go through them this way, even if the sun can't."

"Good idea," said Mrs. Ellison, herself again, patting Melissa's shoulder. "You're a smart girl, Melissa. Now—let's get started on the furniture."

That, and cleaning the mud off the woodburning stove that was the little library's main heat source in winter, proved to be the worst job of all. For three days Melissa and Jed carried books out each morning and in each night and, in between, scraped, scrubbed, and polished, finishing up each day nearly as dark as coal miners and certainly just about as tired. Luckily the sunny weather held and they could take most of the furniture outdoors to clean it.

The hardest piece of furniture both to move and to clean was the huge antique desk that normally stood next to the library's front window. It was elaborately carved with some kind of vine-like decoration, and there was mud, Melissa well knew, scrubbing at it with an old toothbrush, in every twist and curlicue. There was mud packed tightly in every one of the desk's numerous cubbyholes, too, and in all its many drawers.

It was while Melissa was outside scrubbing at just about the last set of viny curlicues that she suddenly noticed a thin trickle of water coming from one side of the desk toward the back. She opened the nearest drawer, but found the mud inside it too dry to have oozed water—and then, just as she was about to call Jed and Mrs. Ellison over to see if they could figure out the source of the leak, a panel on the desk's side popped open and water literally poured out. Melissa reached into what appeared to be a small secret compartment and then recoiled as her fingers met a slimy substance way in the back.

"Jed—Mrs. Ellison," she called, reaching gingerly in again to see if she could pull whatever it was out. "Come here—I think I've found something!"

"Holy cow," said Jed, looking at the sodden, squarish bundle wrapped in brown paper that Melissa drew out with her fingertips. "Looks like . . ." He laughed. "I guess I'm not sure what it looks like except wet!"

"It looks *almost* like a thin pad of paper," said Mrs. Ellison, frowning, "still wrapped from the store."

"Or," said Melissa, loosening one corner of the brown paper, "like pages from a book."

"Careful," said Mrs. Ellison quickly.

Jed gave a low whistle. "Do you suppose . . ." he began. Without finishing, he went to the books that were drying on the lawn, arranged in neat rows conforming to their places on the shelves inside. "RELIGION, FOLKLORE, TOWN HISTORY," he said, ticking off categories as he passed them and bringing *A History of Fours Crossing* back to where Melissa stood, very still now.

"Of course it's probably swollen with all the water," Melissa said as she held the padlike collection of pages against the gap in the edge of the book.

The bundle was a shade thicker than the gap, but just about the right size in all the other directions.

"With that wrapper protecting it, the inside's probably still legible," said Jed, reaching for it—but Mrs. Ellison gasped and grabbed his hand.

"You'll have to wait," she insisted, "until it's drier. If you open it now, you'll probably tear it instead." She glanced at the title on the book's spine and then at the other books drying in the sun. "It's the present that we have to worry about right now," she said, holding out her hands for the bundle Melissa still held. "Not the past."

Melissa gave it to her, realizing that Mrs. Ellison had no way of knowing how important it might be. But she asked Mrs. Ellison to let her or Jed know when the pages had dried enough to examine. As she did, she noticed that Ulfin was lying at the edge of the lawn near the old desk, and that he was watching them intently.

5

Sunday afternoon Jed's father appeared at Gran's in a bright plaid shirt and jeans Melissa was sure he—or Jed—had pressed. "Need anything up to Hiltonville?" he asked. Then he explained proudly that the Board of Selectmen had authorized him to go there the next day for building supplies. The town had hired him, he said, "now that I'm m'self again," to supervise the rebuilding of the two bridges. It was as Gran was congratulating him that Melissa remembered Rhiannon's request for a ride.

"Well, I dunno," he said, absently rubbing Pride and Joy behind the ears; Pride and Joy purred loudly. "Seems an odd one, that woman. Can't see as she's up to much good, keeping to herself so much way up there on Round Top."

"Why, Seth Ellison," Gran said sharply, "I never! After she took Tommy Coffin in when he was lost? You'd not refuse a neighbor who'd helped a neighbor, would you?"

"She even signed up to help the whole town after the flood," put in Melissa.

"Yes," said Seth, "and then never came to do it. Not that

they didn't already have enough people for the jobs she signed up for by the time she put her name down, anyway. Besides, no one could even read it—last name, anyway. Seemed odd, to most folks, that did. Seemed odd, too, the way she held on to Tommy, like, waiting till Jed and Melissa went up there before she let him go."

"She couldn't have let him go out in the storm," said Melissa angrily, "and he *wanted* to stay; she has all these animals . . ."

"Doesn't surprise me that she never came to help," Gran said quickly, "since she's way up the mountain, poor girl, and doesn't seem to have any friends to tell her what's going on. Nor any car, either," she added pointedly, "from what the children say. If that girl's got a relative in Hiltonville, she's got to find some way to get there. It's a mighty long walk."

"Well," grumbled Seth, sounding embarrassed, "I s'pose long as she's got a relative up there, she can't be all *that* much of a stranger. And I guess the Coffins are grateful to her— they say they are, anyway. All right," he said decisively, "but I can only take *her*," he added when Melissa started to ask if she could go along. "The truck's going to be a chockablock full of lumber and bags of cement and hardware on the way back."

"Well, that sounds a bit more neighborly," said Gran, patting Seth's hand and winking at Melissa. "Now, before Mr. Ellison changes his mind, Melissa, maybe you'd best climb up Round Top and tell your friend she can count on a ride tomorrow. Goodness, I hope tomorrow suits her. Seth, I was just about to make some coffee . . ."

Melissa heard the *clack-whoosh, clack-whoosh, clack-whoosh* of the loom as soon as she came through the brush at the top of the first road and then, over it, Linnet's high-pitched bark. The little goat was standing on top of a low box in her pen nibbling hay.

Linnet stopped barking as soon as Melissa knelt to greet her; she licked Melissa's face, wagging her whole back end and her tail in circles. "Helicopter tail," Melissa whispered under the soft flap of her ear. She put her arm around the dog and for a moment knelt quietly in the small clearing, listening to the brook and the peaceful, even sound of the loom from inside. Then Linnet nuzzled her ear, making her laugh.

The loom sounds stopped and Rhiannon, in a plain blue dress instead of her long blue cloak, appeared at the door, one of the gray kittens saucily peeking out from behind her.

"Melissa," she said, with a welcoming smile. "Come in, child. Or better still, I will come out, the sun is so warm today. The kettle is full and already boiling for tea. Wait—" Rhiannon went inside again, scooping up the kitten as she went. Melissa sat down on the cottage's rough stone step and Linnet immediately stretched out in the sun beside her. How much like Ulfin she is, Melissa thought, idly stroking the dog's soft coat, except she's smaller and bouncier and plumper and has longer hair . . .

Her hand, on its way to Linnet's silky ears, got tangled in a loose collar hidden by the dog's hair, and Melissa frowned; had Linnet had a collar on before? She bent closer to look at it; Linnet lay still except for her tail, which thumped slowly against the ground.

Around her neck was a collar made of three gold strands twisted together, almost identical to Ulfin's.

"And here we are," said Rhiannon merrily, coming outside with tea and scones on a tray. "You will see I have butter now, although still no jam." She set the tray down on the ground below the step and went to the brook, from which she took a small brown crockery jar. "And this time the scones are baked," she said, coming back and splitting, then buttering one for Melissa. "Linnet, you have no interest in tea," she added, as the dog pushed herself to a sitting position, nose twitching near the scones.

Linnet gave one final sniff and then moved to the goat pen, thrusting her nose through its wire; the little goat jumped straight up in the air, greeting her exuberantly.

"Linnet wants me to let her friend out," said Rhiannon, getting up and opening the gate. She rubbed the goat's ears affectionately. They stood out at ninety-degree angles from the sides of her head—two signal flags, Melissa thought as they flicked with pleasure.

"Does she have a name?" Melissa asked, laughing as goat and dog circled each other, dancing.

"Not yet," Rhiannon said, her eyes meeting Melissa's more intently than the situation seemed to warrant. "Can you think of one?"

"Daisy," said Melissa, then laughed again, this time in embarrassment. "No, that's a cow, isn't it? And dumb. Let's see. Daphne," she said, the name coming from nowhere. "Diana . . ."

Rhiannon's eyes narrowed, but her mouth smiled. "I was thinking of Dian," she said softly. "Do you like it?"

"Oh, yes," said Melissa. But she felt oddly uncomfortable.

Rhiannon sat down again. "Another scone?" she asked in a normal voice, looking away now.

Melissa ate her second scone in silence, thoughtfully watching Linnet and Dian, who seemed to be working out an elaborate game of tag. Melissa had the distinct feeling that they were doing it more to entertain her than themselves; it made her uncomfortable again, with the same sort of feeling she'd had with Ulfin in the beginning, when he'd seemed almost otherworldly. But that had been because of the missing plate and the hermit; he'd become ordinary, or nearly, once that was sorted out . . .

"May I know your errand?" Rhiannon asked softly, interrupting Melissa's thoughts. "Or did you come just to greet us, and to see my zoo again?"

"No, no," Melissa answered, embarrassed once more. "That is—well, yes, it was partly to—to say hello, of course, but also, yes, there was an errand." She told Rhiannon about Seth's forthcoming trip to Hiltonville. "You said you wanted a ride," she finished. "So I came to say he said you could go with him, if you'd be ready at eight tomorrow morning at the statue on the green—you must've noticed it when you went to the general store . . ." Melissa broke off then, thinking of the discussion about the sign-up sheet.

"I did indeed," said Rhiannon smoothly, "and I thank you. As it is, I must be in Hiltonville tomorrow; I had planned to walk, but this is much better."

"It's over ten miles!" exclaimed Melissa. "That would take forever."

"It would," said Rhiannon, "so I am grateful." She took Melissa's cup. "Stay as long as you like," she said, going into the cottage with the tray. Melissa jumped up; now was her chance to examine Linnet's collar more closely—to see if she had a cipher tag like Ulfin's, too.

The animals had stopped playing and were near the brook, Dian browsing on a low bush while Linnet lapped water. But Linnet turned when Melissa approached and sat, holding out a paw.

"You could be his little sister," Melissa said, taking Linnet's paw and reaching for her collar; Linnet licked her hand.

There was no tag and relief flooded her.

44

"Do you know how to weave?" Rhiannon called, coming back out of the cottage. "Would you like to see my cloth?"

"Oh, yes," Melissa said, genuinely enthusiastic. She joined Rhiannon at the door. "I don't know how, but Gran does. And—and my mother wove some placemats once. She got the pattern from Gran, and . . ."

She broke off suddenly; it was still hard to talk about Mum. For months after her mother had died, Melissa had dreamed about her, dreams that started with happy memories but ended at graveside. The dreams had largely stopped now, and the pain was less. But talking still was hard.

Rhiannon put her hand gently on Melissa's shoulder for a second, and then led her inside.

About ten inches' worth of woven fabric was stretched on the old loom, with blue and brown warp threads leading out of it to the loom's back beam. Spanning the bottom of the fabric was a plain strip of brown with blue flecks, and then came a larger pattern, tiny specks and small elliptical outlines of blue, evenly spaced on a brown background. "It is based on an old Welsh design," Rhiannon explained, showing her how it was done.

"Are you from Wales?" Melissa asked shyly, thinking of how Rhiannon's speech sounded English but not quite.

Rhiannon handed her the shuttle. "Now you do it," she said. "Give it a quick push, as if you were sending a horse home. Now catch it as it comes through—good. Am I from Wales?" she said standing and picking up one of the kittens, who had been eyeing the shuttle with more than casual interest. She smiled and said gently, "Perhaps in a way. From other places, too. Are you from Scotland?"

Melissa looked up, startled enough by the abruptness of Rhiannon's question to let the shuttle fall through to the floor on the other side of the warp. "Well, not exactly," she said, confused, stooping to retrieve the shuttle. "I mean my grandfather, Gran's husband, well, he wasn't Scottish either, I guess, really, but the Dunns came from Scotland; at least I think they did, long ago—Gran makes porridge a lot."

Rhiannon laughed—water over polished pebbles again, like the sound of her name. Melissa, at first angry, suddenly saw how vague her answer had been and laughed also.

"That is how I am Welsh," Rhiannon said, "and Irish, and other things, too—the way you are Scottish." But then her blue eyes turned serious and she put her hand lightly on Melissa's shoulder again. "We are all one," she said quietly. "All one." She held up the kitten; it softly batted Melissa's cheek. "Even him," Rhiannon said, "and the young doe, Dian, and Linnet, and the trees and the sky—all one—and that," she said, smiling at Melissa with her deep and tranquil eyes, "is the first lesson."

Gran's kitchen, streaked with late-afternoon sun, seemed like another world when Melissa got home. Her father, Gran, and Mr.-Ellison-the-Selectman were drinking coffee at the table when she pushed open the back door, still feeling as if she'd come from farther away than Round Top. She tried to walk through inconspicuously, to go up to her room and think, but her father stretched out his hand and said, "Pigeon—good. Would you come and sit down a minute?" He moved Pride and Joy off the remaining chair. "We've been talking—I've got something to ask you."

With a slight feeling of apprehension, Melissa sat down. Her father seemed worried, but she wasn't sure; she had never really known him well, for his work had always kept him away more than at home.

With a glance at Mr. Ellison and then at Gran, her father cleared his throat and then abruptly asked her, "How anxious are you to go back to Boston?"

Melissa, startled, also looked at Gran, but for once Gran's face was as unreadable as her father's. "I—I hadn't thought about it much," she said truthfully. "I guess I sort of thought I could stay till—well, till school's out, anyway. Maybe till fall . . ."

Her father seemed relieved; so did Mr. Ellison. "Then you wouldn't mind," her father said, "if instead of looking for a settled-down job in Boston right away, I—er—went out on the road to do a bit of fund-raising for Fours Crossing?"

"Why—why no," said Melissa, again looking at her grandmother; Gran was smiling now. "No," she repeated, realizing as she said it that it was true. "I'd be happy staying here always. I don't care if we ever go back to Boston."

"Whoa there," her father said, with a wink at Mr. Ellison, who was nodding as if he approved of Melissa's words. "First things first."

Mr. Ellison reached out his big hand and shook Melissa's much smaller one. "Thank you, my dear," he said. "Your daddy told me that his decision about raising money for Fours Crossing would depend entirely on what you said, so you see, the whole village owes you thanks."

"The money's for rebuilding," her father explained, his face grave again, "and for things like having the library's books professionally restored. There are a lot of hidden problems like that, although stained paint and warped doors and mildewed wood are most of what shows now, except for the bridges, of course. The federal government seems to think the flood wasn't bad enough to qualify Fours Crossing for disaster money, and the state . . ."

"The state's got its own troubles." Mr. Ellison chuckled. "Besides, we've always looked after our own in Fours Crossing."

"And," said Stanley Dunn, "now one of your own is looking after you. I'll be proud to raise money for rebuilding Fours Crossing, Henry, and that's a fact."

Mr. Ellison beamed and stood up. "We're mighty beholden to you, Stanley. I think I'll just pop back to the village now and get an announcement put in the paper about your accepting our offer—it'll be a great relief to everyone."

"Does that mean," Melissa asked her father in a small voice when Mr. Ellison had left and Gran was bustling around fixing supper, "that you'll be going away again?"

"Yes, pigeon, it does," he said, kissing her. "And that makes me sad. I'll have to go down to Washington to see if I can change the government's mind about disaster aid before I even start asking other people for money. But I promise that this time I'll write."

"You better mean that, Stanley Dunn," said Gran, breaking eggs into a bowl for one of her splendid omelets. "More than postcards, too, this time."

Melissa's father held up his right hand. "I promise," he said. "Solemnly, truly—whatever other -ly you want."

Melissa smiled back at him. But deep inside, she wasn't quite sure she could count on him, and she wished fervently that he would stay.

6

Melissa's father did write, and he also phoned, which made him seem a lot less far away.

Despite the flood's vestiges, once school started again life was much easier in the village than Melissa had ever known it—no snow to shovel, no fuel and food shortages to worry about, and much, much warmer weather. Melissa was able to go to school in just a light jacket, instead of the mittens, scarves, thick sweaters, and hats she was used to. And she could walk in ordinary shoes—no boots, no snowshoes. All around now there were signs of spring. Melissa discovered a wonderful place by the river, where it formed a little pool below the depot, with peepers, bright-green skunk cabbage, and a nest of duck eggs—and once, a whole flock of tiny, newly hatched turtles—pebbles on legs, they looked like.

Gran suddenly found what seemed like a million spring chores to do, both outside and in. Aside from one afternoon when Melissa helped her plant lettuce and peas—"Late," Gran told her, "but the ground's been too boggy till now"—Melissa hardly saw her except at meals.

There was one very difficult afternoon, though, which

Melissa went through in a near-daze, when a Mr. Davis, having had a session with Jed earlier, sat for several hours in Gran's kitchen, talking with Melissa about the hermit and the kidnapping in preparation for the hermit's trial, which was to be held soon. Mr. Davis, who had white hair and a large red face and seemed inclined to bluster, was the district attorney. "That means I'm the prosecutor," he explained in a loud, cheerful voice, accepting a cup of coffee and a home-made doughnut from Gran. "I'm the chap who's going to try to show that Mr. Eli John Dunn—er—the hermit—is guilty. And you, little lady, and your friend Jed, can help me do it, just by answering the questions I'll ask you in court. They'll mostly be about those two days that the hermit kept you in the root cellar. Now . . ."

"Excuse me," Gran interrupted while Melissa stared blindly into her untouched cup of tea, wishing herself far away, "but just when will the trial be?"

"Soon," Mr. Davis answered. "Surprisingly soon, in fact. The court calendar's clear. Besides," he boomed, "this is the biggest case we've had in these parts for years." He took a big bite of doughnut and munched for a moment in silence; not *very* soon, Melissa hoped, dreading having to face the hermit again, even in a courtroom.

"Yes," Mr. Davis went on, "the defense attorney—O'Callahan's his name—Mr. O'Callahan's having some psychiatrists examine the hermit; he's going to try to show that he's insane. Soon as that's over, we can go ahead. Ordinarily, of course"—here Mr. Davis took a swallow of coffee, washing down the last of the doughnut —"ordinarily, the whole process would take months, but, well, the hermit's been deteriorating, I hear . . ."

Melissa looked up, wondering just what Mr. Davis meant by that. But before she could ask, Gran said, "Well, the sooner the better." She patted Melissa's hand. "All we want is to put that awful time behind us, don't we, Melissa?"

Melissa nodded, and Mr. Davis smiled, pushing his cup aside and reaching into his briefcase for a thick pad of paper and a pen. "Well, it'll be over soon enough," he said. "Luckily we have our own ways of doing things in these parts. If we were down in Concord—or in Boston, where you come from, Melissa, don't you?—this would drag on well into winter and beyond. Now then, Melissa . . ."

Slowly, but in a voice that grew until soon it was loud enough to fill Gran's kitchen, Mr. Davis went through the questions he planned to ask Melissa at the trial. Melissa found herself answering almost in monosyllables until Mr. Davis, lowering his voice to a more conversational level, said, "You'd be a dream come true for most lawyers, young lady, because you don't embroider the truth, but you can tell more than you're telling, I'm sure. Now—once more—that second morning in the root cellar . . ."

"It's just that I want to forget it," Melissa told Gran when at last Mr. Davis had left.

"I know, lambie," Gran said, hugging her. "And I wish you could. But remember what Mr. Davis said: the more you can recollect about what happened, the more chance there is that he'll be able to get the hermit put where he can't do anyone harm again."

Melissa nodded, knowing Gran was right, and that night she forced herself to make a list of everything that had happened from the time the hermit had kidnapped them till the time they were rescued. Later, she woke up, trembling, from a dream in which she remembered even more, and she got out of bed and added to her list.

It would have been easier if she'd been able to talk with Jed about her memories, and about the trial. But he was too busy; eighth-grade graduation—his—had been rescheduled for Midsummer Day, June 21, because of time lost during the snowbound winter and the flood. That meant exams were coming up, and as soon as the dates were posted, Jed started studying for them with a diligence that was new to Melissa. Tommy was busy, too, with a new village baseball team Frank Grange of the Highway Department had organized, and so Melissa, to keep from thinking about seeing the hermit again, offered to take care of Rhiannon's storm waifs while Rhiannon was away doing whatever it was she did in Hiltonville. It was hard work—cages to clean, food and water to distribute, wounds to dress, bandages to change—but rewarding, for soon the wild animals as well as the kittens seemed to recognize and greet her, especially the young sparrow hawk, who, now that he was no longer bedraggled, looked very handsome, with blue wings and a jaunty blue-and-rust-colored cap that ended in a sleek point above his beak.

Even with the threat of the trial, Fours Crossing seemed so peaceful to Melissa, especially when she was with Rhiannon's animals, that if anyone had told her that something ugly was beginning to grow under the village's friendly exterior, she would have found it hard to believe—and yet, that was exactly what was happening. It began, the way ugliness often does, with the faintest of whispers, like wind blowing across a field of dry grass. But before long, as if someone had dropped a lighted match in that field and the wind had fanned it, the whispers grew louder, spreading as fast as raging flames.

The first whisper came one balmy day when Melissa passed some six- or seven-year-old children chanting jump-rope rhymes in the schoolyard:

Witchy, witchy, witchy.
Twitchy, twitchy, twitchy.

Twitch a witch, witch a twitch,
Her—name—is—Rhi—an—non!

Horrified, Melissa seized the last child lined up to jump and demanded, "Where did you learn that?"

The child just shrugged and said, "It's only a rhyme." Another child, glancing up, started on "A, my name is Alice," and Melissa tried to forget the incident. But later she heard the rhyme again, and the name was always the same.

Then one afternoon Melissa went to the general store for Gran and saw Rhiannon there, carrying a large bag of flour to the counter. Melissa was about to greet her when Mr. Titus turned away from Rhiannon, who was next, and said, "Hello, Melissa, what can I do for you?" It wasn't until Melissa said, "This lady is ahead of me," that Mr. Titus seemed to notice Rhiannon at all. And as Rhiannon and Melissa were leaving and Melissa was chattering about anything at all to hide her embarrassment, a woman coming into the store with a boy of about eight pulled the child roughly to her other side, putting herself between Rhiannon and him.

Well, Melissa said to herself, maybe there was something I didn't see—maybe there was a bee or something. Or maybe the little boy had been bad and she was scolding him.

But the ugliness went on growing.

"Well, all I can say is, she hasn't gotten any mail since she's been here," Melissa heard Mrs. Dupres, the postmistress, say in a low voice to a woman customer when Melissa went in to mail a letter to her father. "Of course, how could she, with no last name as far as anyone knows, at least none anyone could read on that cleanup list she signed and then never acted on, and . . . Yes, dear, may I help you?"

"I'd like a stamp for this, please," Melissa said, and then, as casually as she could, she asked, "Who hasn't gotten any mail?"

"Oh, that stranger-woman," said Mrs. Dupres, while the customer nodded in a gossipy way. "The one who kept Tommy Coffin up there on Round Top without telling anyone the night of the flood. *Such* an odd creature—really, I wonder your grandmother lets you visit her so much. You do go up there often, dear, don't you, after school?"

"Yes," said Melissa defiantly, "I do. I go to take care of the animals she saved from the flood—the way she saved Tommy —while she's in Hiltonville and can't be there herself."

"Oh, yes," said the other woman, saccharine-sweet. "She goes to Hiltonville often, doesn't she? And I hear Seth Ellison's been getting up at the crack of dawn every day to drive her there. *And* going back at the end of the day to fetch her." She exchanged a knowing smile with Mrs. Dupres.

Feeling a little sick, Melissa hurried out of the post office.

But the worst time of all, at the beginning anyway, was Saturday morning, when Melissa passed Seth Ellison and two other men putting the finishing touches on the new depot bridge.

"Tired from last night, eh, Seth?" said one of the men, winking at the other and jabbing him in the ribs with a crooked elbow. "Hear you didn't get back from Hiltonville till mighty late."

"I had dinner with our neighbor from Round Top," Seth said evenly—but Melissa, who decided it would be better to continue walking than to stop and say good morning, could see the anger in his eyes as she passed.

"Oh-ho," said the other man, with a grin. "Pretty nice little piece, that Rhiannon, eh, Seth?"

"I wouldn't know," Seth said, driving a spike into the bridge with two mighty blows of his hammer. "Good morning, Melissa," he said loudly.

"Good morning, Mr. Ellison," Melissa said, smiling warmly at him but pointedly ignoring the others.

Could it be true? It had never even occurred to Melissa to question Rhiannon's relationship with Jed's father.

"So what if it is true," Tommy said the next day when he was helping Melissa look for birds' nests in the field behind Gran's house before the mowers came. "Mr. Ellison's wife's been dead for years. So what if he likes Rhiannon? Gee," Tommy said, looking up at Melissa, his hands deep in the already surprisingly tall grass, "what if they got married or something? Then Jed'd have a mother."

"Stepmother," Melissa corrected, feeling sure that Jed wouldn't like that idea at all.

"Hmm." Tommy took off his acorn cap and rubbed the back of his neck with it. "Well, at least then he wouldn't have to do all the cooking and cleaning and stuff anymore." He stuffed the cap into his back pocket.

"He hasn't had to do all of that anyway, since Mr. Ellison stopped drinking," Melissa said testily. "Look out, Tom, there's a nest; you almost stepped on it."

"Sorry," said Tommy, carefully pounding in a tall stake that would tell the mowers to cut around the small bundle of grass, weeds, and root-twigs that protected three brown-spotted, grayish eggs.

That night, doing dishes with Gran, Melissa said moodily, "I think it's rotten the way people talk about other people."

"What people, lambie?"

"Oh, everyone. Talking about other people behind their backs." Melissa shook out her towel vigorously and reached for a drier one. "It isn't right."

"Well," said Gran, scrubbing a saucepan, "you're right, it isn't. But in a small town . . ."

"I never heard anyone here talk about anyone before," Melissa said. "Not in the time I've been here."

"For most of that time," said Gran, "all anyone could think of was the snow. And there were no strangers in town, lambie, except you, and since you're my granddaughter, you don't quite count as a stranger. Is it that Rhiannon woman you mean?"

"She's not 'that Rhiannon woman,' " Melissa said crossly. "She's just Rhiannon, and she's my friend."

"I wonder," said Gran, handing Melissa the saucepan, "what her last name is. Do you know?"

"No," said Melissa uncomfortably. "I don't. And I don't see why everyone thinks it's so important."

"Well," said Gran, "seems to me if folks knew just the least little bit more about her, they might not be so suspicious." She pulled the stopper out of the sink and seemed intent for a moment on the soapy water gurgling down. "Melissa," she said finally, "in a place as little as Fours Crossing, everyone knows a good deal about everyone else. Good things and bad. The beauty of it is, folks also still say good morning and good night to each other and help each other out, no matter what they know—most times, anyway. But when someone doesn't even tell their last name—well, I guess folks feel cheated."

"She wrote it down," said Melissa belligerently. "It's not her fault if no one could read it."

But even though Gran smiled and seemed content with that, Melissa went to bed wondering about it all the same.

"Last name," said Rhiannon, her laugh rippling musically as she and Melissa waded in the brook to cool off on one of the rare afternoons when Rhiannon wasn't in Hiltonville. "Well, let me see. Jones?"

For the second time since she'd known Rhiannon, Melissa

felt angry at her. And this time a little corner of suspicion edged its way into her mind. "What do you mean, 'Let me see'?" she asked. "Is your last name Jones or isn't it?"

Rhiannon looked sadly away. "Oh, Melissa," she said softly. For a moment she was silent, and then she smiled, although still sadly. "Jones, then. Rhiannon Jones." She held out her slender hand and waggled it at Melissa. "How do you do?" she said, her smile wry now. "Melissa Dunn, I believe? My name is Rhiannon Jones. What a pleasure to meet you."

Impulsively, Melissa threw her arms around Rhiannon and hugged her close. "I'm sorry," she whispered, though she wasn't quite sure why. "Rhiannon, I'm so sorry!"

The next afternoon Melissa made a point of going into the general store and asking in a loud voice, "Has Miss Jones been in today? Miss *Rhiannon* Jones?"

Mr. Titus looked at her over his spectacles. "Jones, eh? That her last name?"

"Why, yes," said Melissa airily, feigning astonishment. "Didn't you know?"

"Well," Mr. Titus said, carefully polishing the glass front of one of his display cases, "only time I saw it written, 'twasn't done so's anyone could read it. Jones, eh? Course, you can't be dead sure with a name like Jones. Jones and Smith, I always say, can't quite trust 'em . . ."

"*Ohhhh!*" Melissa said, exasperated, and ran out of the store without buying anything—ran almost full force into Jed, who was running himself, looking as if he'd sooner crash into anyone in his path than say hello.

"Jed Ellison," Melissa said as he tried to push past her, "can't you even say excuse me? Here you've had your nose in your books all this time, and now you can't even . . ."

But Jed elbowed her aside. "Leave me alone, Melissa," he said in an oddly choked voice.

Melissa grabbed his arm and forced him to turn around. His none-too-clean face was suspiciously streaked under the eyes and his hands were fists; his mouth was in a tight, thin line. With a sharp motion of his elbow, he thrust Melissa aside and broke into a run again.

It was then that Melissa noticed the blood on his back.

7

Melissa, stunned, waited till Jed was out of sight. Then she headed slowly out of the village and up to Gran's, for if what she suspected was true, she knew Jed would probably go there.

And sure enough, when she cautiously pushed open the kitchen door, there was Jed, his shirt off, sitting backward on a chair by the sink, while Gran gently sponged his back. He wasn't crying, exactly, but Melissa could see it was an effort for him not to.

"A little more washing, laddie," Gran was saying softly, as if to a very young child. "Just to make sure it's good and clean. Then some of the ointment—it's lucky I had some left, isn't it?"

"I guess, Miz Dunn," Jed answered through clenched teeth. "Though I'd thought maybe we wouldn't need it anymore."

Melissa closed the door as quietly as she could—and then opened it to let in Ulfin, who, panting, went right to Jed and licked his hand, then lay next to him, watching every move Gran made. Melissa wondered if she should try to go straight through the kitchen pretending she didn't see Jed there. But that would be nearly impossible—and then he saw her anyway, and gave her such a brave, ironic smile that she went to him quickly and took both his hands. "Oh, Jed," she said, gripping hard. She winced when she looked over his shoulder and saw the two ragged welts on his back as Gran began drying it with gentle pats of a clean towel. "Was it . . ."

Jed, grimacing a little, nodded. "I got—home," he said between pats, "and caught him. He was—sitting in his chair by—the woodstove and there was the—bottle next to him." He looked up at Gran and freed his hands from Melissa's. "It was only about half full, so I knew he'd been at it awhile."

"And you said something," said Gran grimly, uncapping the ointment. Its pungent smell made Melissa wrinkle her nose.

"Of course I did!" Jed said indignantly. "He'd promised not to drink anymore. But he got mad, said he'd drink if he wanted to—that he was my father, not me his. And then he grabbed me and—well, you know."

"Belt buckle?" Gran asked, rubbing ointment in.

Jed nodded, gritting his teeth. "Good thing for him that Ulfin wasn't there," he said, reaching down to pat the dog, who eased himself up and carefully leaned against Jed, as if to give him support against the pain.

"Once more, Jed," said Gran, "and I am going to have to say something to Chief Dupres. Or Mr. Savage."

Mr. Savage—Joan's father—was a lawyer whom Gran called on sometimes; he had already agreed, Gran had told Melissa, to help explain things during the hermit's trial if he had time.

"No need to tell them, Miz Dunn," Jed said. "It's okay. I figure on leaving, anyway."

Gran put down the ointment and went around to the front of Jed's chair.

"Leaving?" Melissa said.

"Just what do you mean by that, Jethro Ellison?" Gran said at the same time.

"What I said," Jed answered, struggling into his shirt; Ulfin watched, ears forward expectantly. "I'm fourteen now, Miz Dunn, and—well, I guess I can look after myself. Dad's been different lately, since that Rhiannon woman came—since he's been driving her to Hiltonville. I figure it was what folks've been saying about them that made him drink again and—well, if that's the way things are going to be, I'm not going to stay around to watch, that's all."

"But, Jed . . ." Melissa began. Gran motioned her to be quiet.

"Where were you planning on going?" Gran asked casually.

"Oh," Jed answered, just as casually, "I thought I'd go up to Hiltonville and see if I can get work in one of the stores there."

"Umm," said Gran. "And I suppose get yourself a hotel room."

"Right," he answered. "Or maybe a place in one of those rooming houses. They're cheaper, I guess."

"Stand up," Gran said abruptly.

"Huh?"

"Stand up," she repeated, and when he did, she stepped over Ulfin and circled Jed, her head on one side as if, Melissa thought, he were a horse she was thinking of buying.

"Well," said Gran doubtfully, "I don't know, Jed; really, I don't."

"Don't know what?" he asked, obviously confused.

"How you're going to pass for sixteen," she said. "Someone sees you working—if anyone'll hire you without suspecting—they'll start wondering why you're not in school. Probably send you right back . . ."

"I'll tell 'em I go to a private school," Jed said stubbornly.

"They get out earlier. Or I'll go farther away than Hiltonville —Boston, maybe. Or New York. They don't care in cities. Maybe Canada—Montreal."

"Oh, Jed, don't go!" Melissa said, caring too much to hold back. "Please don't. I—I'd miss you. Tommy'd miss you. So would Gran," she said; Gran nodded. "And your dad would too, Jed. You know how miserable Tommy said he was when the hermit had us; you know how he helped find us. It was you your father was looking for; he loves you, Jed; he's just— just . . ." Melissa looked helplessly at Gran and then at Ulfin, whose tail brushed the floor once, softly.

"Your dad's weak, Jethro," said Gran softly. "That's a hard truth, but truth it is."

"He can't even take a little kidding," Jed said bitterly, turning away. "I mean if he likes that woman, which I hope he doesn't, he ought to be able to take a little kidding. Especially since she's—well, people say she's . . ." His voice trailed off.

"She's what?" Gran asked.

Jed suddenly turned bright red; he stooped, fiddling with Ulfin's collar.

"Melissa," said Gran apologetically, "isn't it time to feed the chickens?"

"No!" Melissa protested. "Gran, no, it's . . ."

"She can stay," Jed said, straightening up again. "She spends all her time up there; she ought to hear it, too. She thinks Rhiannon's good. Well," he said, turning on Melissa furiously, "she's not, if what they're saying is true. She's got my dad so—bewitched that he spends every night talking in his sleep and saying my mother's name like a crazy man. And drinking, too, now. At least he's only drinking at night, so far. But they're saying she's some kind of—of loose woman and that he's taken up with her. He won't tell anyone why she goes to Hiltonville, but he takes longer and longer each time to come home when he goes to get her, and then the last couple nights when he's come in he's gone right for the bottle. Anyone can see that she . . ."

"Jed," said Gran, "you're believing gossip. I thought you were smarter than that. And," Gran said softly, "I believe you're even jealous. Your dad's been a lonely man since your mother died. If he's finally interested in a woman, well, I say that's fine. Maybe he's trying to work it out in his mind—maybe he can't quite let your mother go. But, Jed, listen. If I'd been a younger woman, I'd maybe have married again, after my husband died. It wouldn't have meant that I didn't love my husband, just that I was lonely without him. I was, Jed, and I would have been even if I'd had a child at home, the way your dad has you."

"I—I know," Jed said miserably. "But why *that* woman? Why a stranger?"

"Well," said Gran thoughtfully, washing the ointment off her hands, "there aren't very many unmarried women in Fours Crossing, I s'pose is part of it. And sometimes it's easier to take up with someone brand new. Jed," she said, turning back to face him, "suppose I invite Rhiannon to tea? It's time I was neighborly toward her. And I'm a pretty good judge of character."

"Well . . ." said Jed.

"I promise I'll give you a full and honest opinion," said Gran, "if you promise not to do anything foolish until afterward. Agreed?"

Jed shrugged. "I guess."

"Good," said Gran briskly. "Now—since last I heard there weren't any phones on Round Top, why don't you and Melissa and Ulfin go up there and say I send my regards and would Rhiannon come to tea tomorrow afternoon, or whenever she can if that isn't convenient?"

The next afternoon was rainy, but it was a warm rain this time, spring-like and gentle, and Melissa walked home from school slowly, savoring it. She was also trying to give Gran as much time as possible alone with Rhiannon. She'd left Jed in the library, a math book—his worst subject—propped up in front of him. Each time she'd seen him that day in school, he'd acted as if nothing unusual was happening, but she could see the nervousness underneath by the way he kept looking at his watch and, at lunch, by the way he hardly ate.

Melissa took off her boots and raincoat as quietly as she could in the kitchen and then listened for a moment in the hall before going into the living room. Gran had a fire going —she could hear its cozy crackling—and the two women seemed to be talking about recipes. "Then you stir it well," she heard Gran saying, "and *my* mother always used to add more cream of tartar, but I don't think it's needed— Oh, Melissa," Gran said, looking up as Melissa went in, "there you are. There's just about one cup left in the pot. Come to the fire and dry off."

"Hello, Melissa," Rhiannon said, smiling.

"Hi," Melissa said. Rhiannon was wearing a softly muted brown plaid skirt and a tan blouse with long, full sleeves. She looked more like a young schoolteacher or office worker than —than what? Melissa wondered, pouring herself some tea.

"Rhiannon's been telling me about her weaving," said Gran, passing Melissa the sugar. "We were just exchanging dye recipes."

Melissa moved Pride and Joy from a chair near the fire and sat down, careful to keep her teacup level on its saucer.

"Mmm," she said, sipping tea and trying to smile at Rhiannon at the same time. "She's got this wonderful big loom, Gran. Did you tell her about it, Rhiannon?"

"Not yet," Rhiannon said, and turned to Gran. "It was there when I found the little cottage—I wonder whose it was." She smiled back at Melissa. "There were a few pieces missing, but otherwise it was fine, although it looked as if it had not been used for many years; it was covered with cobwebs."

"And you're using it now, are you, for the shawl you were telling me about?" Gran asked, passing Melissa the plate of Toll House cookies. "A nice blue and a brown, you said?"

Rhiannon smiled again. "Yes," she said. "I found a rather good wool shop on my way here. The Sheared Sheep, it is called. Do you know it?"

Gran laughed. "No, I don't think so," she said, "but then, I run more to carpentry than handicrafts these days."

"Yes," said Rhiannon smoothly. "Mr. Ellison—he so kindly has been my chauffeur, you might say, since I arrived—Mr. Ellison was saying you used to teach carpentry—taught him when he was a boy, I think he said?"

Gran smiled. "Land, that was years ago! He was my prize pupil. And," she said, putting down her cup, "I've been so happy to see him working at it again. He'd stopped for a while, you know."

"Yes," said Rhiannon. "I believe he had some trouble with drink after his wife died."

Melissa hid behind her teacup. It was as if Gran and Rhiannon were sparring with each other, each trying to find out what the other knew. She'd never seen Gran like this and wasn't sure she liked it. But it's for Jed, she kept telling herself; Mr. Ellison, too, maybe . . .

"My grandmother was a bit of a weaver," said Gran, deftly

changing the subject. "I have a few of her things, tablecloths and dish towels, mostly. But there's a fine old tapestry of hers in the dining room. Perhaps you'd like to see it?"

"I would indeed," said Rhiannon, putting down her cup. "Very much."

Melissa took a final swallow of tea and then followed the two women into the dining room. It was her favorite room in Gran's house aside from her own bedroom, which was right above it, snuggled next to the chimney. It was the oldest room, too, Gran had explained soon after Melissa arrived in Fours Crossing; it had been built back in the late 1600s by the village's first settlers. The rest of the house had been built around and on top of it.

Rhiannon and Gran were standing in front of the tapestry, a bright and complicated pattern of reds, blues, yellows, and greens. "My," said Rhiannon, examining it closely, "what a fine piece of work. May I touch it?"

"Certainly," Gran said. "I know you'll be careful—it's so old . . ."

Rhiannon, gently fingering the tapestry, moved to one side as if to catch the light better on its intricately woven threads. But then, so purposefully it was hard for Melissa to believe it was accidental, she dropped her hand, looking toward the wall where the plates hung, and exclaimed, "Oh, but these—these are lovely also, and even older, are they not?" She crossed quickly to them and dipped her head ever so slightly—the way people do in church, Melissa thought afterward, wondering how to describe it to Jed, or before a shrine.

"It must have been one of these that was stolen," Rhiannon said, glancing at Melissa, who nodded, though she had the sudden distinct feeling that Rhiannon had no need of an answer, that she knew more about the plates, despite her questions, than Gran did.

"Yes, this one," said Gran, pointing to the spring plate, and apparently not thinking it odd that Rhiannon's focus had changed so quickly. "And you're right that they're older than the tapestry. But I don't think they're as old as they look. I've always thought they might be copies of something older still. They've been here as long as the house has. According to Melissa's great-grandfather, they came to this country with the first Dunns, so that would make them at least three hundred years old. Melissa can tell you about the robbery; I'll just clear away the tea things."

As Gran left the room, Rhiannon raised a finger and traced the carvings on one of the plates—the summer plate, Melissa realized, the one with the stylized rowan leaves on it and the cipher letters spelling SOMMER. She touched it reverently, and as if it were something she knew well.

Then she turned to Melissa and smiled. "It is this one now," she said. More urgently, her smile fading, she said, "Feel how warm it is."

A little reluctantly, Melissa reached up to the plate and felt the cipher letters, the leaves, the L-shaped groove that formed one quarter of a cross when combined with the grooves on the other three plates—a plate for each of the four seasons and a circle containing an even-sided cross for the year, as she and Jed had figured out not so long ago.

It was true; the summer plate was warm. And, as Rhiannon went back to the living room and started talking with Gran about thread counts and warps as if nothing had happened, Melissa reached up and touched the other three plates. They were room temperature, the same as the walls.

8

"A nice young woman," Gran said, giving Jed her "report" outside the back door after school the next day. "A little strange, maybe, but she told me she's lived alone most of her life, and people who spend a lot of time alone often have trouble being comfortable with other folks. I imagine that's why she keeps so much to herself. As to her not helping out— well, I was right. No one told her when to go; she was willing enough. She admires your father greatly, Jed, and she's no loose woman, as I'll certainly say to anyone who so much as breathes any nonsense like that in my presence." With that, Gran picked up her feed bucket from the back steps and went off to the henhouse; Melissa took Jed into the dining room and told him about Rhiannon's asking her to touch the plate, which was no warmer than the others now.

"We still don't know what she does in Hiltonville," Jed said, looking thoughtfully up at the plates when Melissa had finished.

"Maybe," said Melissa tentatively, "it's none of our business."

Jed shook his head; Melissa saw him wince as his shirt

rubbed against his back. "I think it is," he said. "Especially now." He touched the summer plate again, and then the others.

"What do you mean?"

Jed pulled his shirt out a bit. "First of all, even if it isn't true that she's—well, not good—and I don't know it isn't—why would Dad have gotten drunk?"

"Because of the stupid gossip," Melissa said heatedly. "You pretty much said that yourself. That'd be enough to make anyone drink, especially if it's all lies!"

"Well," Jed said stubbornly, "we don't know that what people are saying *is* all lies, do we?" He turned to Melissa. "Look, maybe your gran's right that he needs someone. But the thing is, I'm not sure she's good for him. The other thing is that I'm not sure she's any good at all."

"Oh, come on. I like her. Tommy likes her."

"You two are just about the only ones who do. And your gran. But—well, remember your gran was so sorry for the hermit she almost liked him."

"She did not!" Melissa said angrily. "Sorry for isn't the same as liking."

"Well, which is it for the witch woman, then?" asked Jed defiantly.

Melissa stomped angrily out of the room.

"Look, I'm sorry," he said, following her. "It's what the little kids call her. Witchy, witchy, witchy."

"I know!" Melissa shouted, wheeling to face him. "Now who's telling rumors and gossiping? You should be ashamed of yourself, Jed Ellison!"

"The plate," he said insistently. "Why was the plate warm?"

"How should I know? Maybe it was just my imagination. I expected something, the way she asked me to touch it. But maybe there wasn't anything."

"Then *why* did she want you to touch it? Why did she come here when the rain did? Why does she live up there on Round Top with all those animals? And why does she go to Hiltonville so much?"

"I don't know." Melissa pushed aside the sudden picture of Linnet's collar and the sound of Rhiannon's singing. "I don't know. But I don't see why people can't have faith in someone even if they're a little different from other people."

"Well," said Jed stubbornly, "I'm going to find out what she does in Hiltonville. If you want to come, you can. The next time Dad says he's going to drive her there, I'm going to stow away in his truck or hitchhike or ride my bike or something."

The next time, it turned out, was Saturday, so it was easy for Melissa to convince Gran to let her go on an early-morning bike ride with Jed. She told herself she was going along to make sure Jed was fair, rather than out of disloyalty to Rhiannon. But secretly she knew she was just as curious as he was. It would be fun, too, to see Hiltonville at last.

Gran packed a picnic lunch for two and let Melissa use her old bike, which she'd kept in good repair; she still used it herself for short errands in nice weather, she said, to keep in shape.

They started early, in order to get to Hiltonville well before Rhiannon and Seth. There was only one road into the small mountain town from Fours Crossing, Jed explained, so all they'd have to do would be find a place to hide near the town line and they'd be able to see Seth's pickup truck when it arrived and follow it.

It was going to be a beautiful late-spring day, warm and clear, maybe even hot. Despite the somewhat clandestine nature of their errand, Melissa felt lighthearted as she pedaled along behind Jed out of the village. The sun touched Round Top with pink as it climbed higher in the pale-blue sky—this must be sky-blue-pink, Melissa thought, smiling as a single bird trilled in the meadow ahead, waking others, who answered. The air was fresh and smelled of newly cut grass, of earth, of brook and river water; they stopped for a while beside a stream to rest. When they started up again, Melissa threw back her head in exhilaration, wanting to join the birds in singing—but then Jed called over his shoulder, "We'd best speed up," and Melissa nodded, put her head down, and pedaled faster. The meadow sped by, with Round Top curving gently above it; then came a patch of woods, then a large farm with cows just being turned out to pasture. Smoke curled lazily from the farmhouse chimney, and a boy herding the cows returned their wave and called off the wiry black-and-white sheep dog that ran out to the road barking. Soon a farmer turned into the main road from a small side one, driving a slow tractor, which they passed, again exchanging waves. Then there was a truck ahead of them, and gradually more and more cars. "Folks going to work in Hiltonville," Jed said after the fourth one passed them, "or to shop; we'd better hurry."

Finally, after an especially exhausting hill, the road dipped into a valley and Melissa could see, before they descended, a cluster of rooftops, chimneys, and, to one side, the double ribbon of the railroad track, with smoke from a freight engine puffing into the sky. "Hiltonville," Jed said as they went over the brow of the hill. "Be ready to brake; this hill's even steeper than it looks."

It was; Melissa found herself using both brakes, gripping the handle for the back one firmly and cautiously squeezing the front one now and then when the back seemed in danger of slipping. Then the road abruptly leveled off. There was a small white house, with a brick one beyond, then a gas station, and ahead, more houses closer together, leading onto what was clearly a main street, lined with shops.

"Not quite Boston, I bet." Jed hopped off his bike opposite the gas station, near a cluster of low-branched evergreen trees.

"Not quite," said Melissa, jumping off her bike, too, and rubbing her legs; her knees felt like stretched rubber bands. "Whew! I sure hope we can go slower on the way home. How's your back?"

"A bit scratchy," he admitted. "I wouldn't mind going slower myself. We could make some side trips, if you want. There's a terrific lake—we should've brought bathing suits."

"It's only the end of May," Melissa reminded him, wondering silently and then out loud if a lake this far north in New Hampshire and this high up in the mountains would still be too cold for swimming, especially after such a bad winter.

"You're right," he said reluctantly, then grinned and added, "Pretty smart for city folks, aren't you? It'd probably sting my back, too, come to think of it. Is there anything besides sandwiches in that lunch bag?"

"I don't know," said Melissa, rummaging in her bike basket. "Yes. Have a doughnut."

They sat under the trees munching Gran's homemade doughnuts, hidden from the road by branches but still able to see the cars that passed. Jed seemed to be in a better mood than he'd been in for some time—maybe, thought Melissa, because he's finally doing something instead of brooding . . .

Suddenly Jed stiffened and put his hand on her arm. "I think I hear Dad's truck," he said. "Get ready to move."

Melissa stood up carefully so she wouldn't disturb their screen of evergreen branches, and stuffed the lunch bag back into her basket. Jed watched the road, his hands gripping the handlebars of his bike and his feet in position to spring on.

72

"We'll have to give them a lead," he said tensely, "so Dad won't recognize us in the mirror."

Melissa nodded. A red-and-white truck shot by and Jed started counting. At ten, he said, "Come on!" and sprang onto his bike; they both sped out onto the road. Melissa could just make out the truck ahead of them—going fast, as if its occupants were late for something.

Hiltonville's main street was thick with cars now, and soon branched out, forming the four sides of a square, with official-looking buildings lining one side and a grassy, parklike green in the center. A traffic policeman held up his hand just after the truck went past, forcing Jed and Melissa to stop. "Rats!" Jed exclaimed under his breath. "We'll lose them now, for sure."

But the truck, instead of going on, pulled up in front of one of the official-looking buildings, and Rhiannon got out. With a wave to Seth, she ran up the steps and disappeared inside. Simultaneously, the policeman motioned Jed and Melissa forward. As the truck drove around the square and back toward Fours Crossing, Jed pulled Melissa quickly behind a parked car.

"I wonder if they saw us," Melissa said when the truck had gone by and they came out into the open again.

"I don't think so," said Jed. "Dad would've stopped. Come on!"

Jed pedaled furiously up to some bike racks in front of the building Rhiannon had entered, thrust his bike into the nearest slot, and ran up the steps in almost one motion. Melissa followed, hoping there was no need to lock the bikes as there certainly would have been at home. But then in most of Boston there wouldn't even have been bike racks, not in front of such an important-looking building, anyway.

It was, Melissa realized as she followed Jed up the stone

steps, the largest building she had seen since she'd left home in March—at least five stories high, brick, with neat rows of windows lined up like soldiers on parade. At the top of the steps were heavy glass doors framed in brass; the lobby inside was cavernous and dimly lit, with a gleaming, slippery marble floor. A discreet black-and-white sign across the lobby listed what seemed to be offices and their locations.

Melissa and Jed stood near the door for a moment at a loss as to where to start looking. Rhiannon was nowhere to be seen; in fact, the lobby was empty except for a small group of people waiting for an elevator at one end and a uniformed guard who now came toward them from the other.

"Yes?" he said, looking down at them a bit severely, as if the building were somehow his and they were the first other people who had ever ventured inside. "May I help you?"

"Well," Jed began, "I guess. That is . . ."

"We're looking for a lady," Melissa said, trying a smile on the man, who didn't respond. "She—er—she just came in. She's tall—long black hair and very blue eyes and she—what was she wearing, Jed?"

Jed shrugged; he was squinting at the sign, apparently trying to read it.

"Well," said Melissa, "I'm not sure I actually saw what she was wearing this morning, but she does have this blue—well, a sort of cape thing that she often wears and maybe . . ."

The guard's mouth twitched a little. "And what might your business be?" he asked gravely.

"Well, we, er . . ." Melissa stammered. "We just . . ."

"We have a message for her," Jed said smoothly.

"There is a lady a bit like that who comes in," said the guard dubiously. "You'd best wait here for her, though. Sometimes she's here for quite a while. Not lately, though. Lately she's been in and out, like." He gestured to a bench near the elevator and wandered over to the main door.

"Helpful, wasn't he?" Melissa said. "You'd think he could at least have told us . . . What is it, Jed?" She followed him across the lobby to the sign; he pointed to an entry at the bottom:

HILTONVILLE COUNTY JAIL . . . . *Basement*

Melissa's stomach turned uncomfortably over. "But we don't . . ." she began.

Jed glanced at the guard, whose back was to them now as he talked to a man who had just come in with a briefcase. Jed inclined his head toward a door near the elevator. STAIRS, it said over it in large black letters. "Come on," he said, grabbing Melissa's hand. "Quick, before old pasty-face turns around."

The stairs were dark and rather narrow. Jed pulled Melissa down them so quickly that they both almost ran straight into a heavy wall of iron grillwork that blocked the landing at the bottom. There was a metal door in the grillwork, closed and bolted with a formidable lock. Beyond the landing were two or three steps leading into a dark corridor.

Jed let out his breath in an angry, impatient wheeze.

Melissa pointed to the landing, in one corner of which were a desk and a chair. "Another guard, I'll bet," she whispered. "Maybe he'll know."

"Well, he's not here to ask," Jed said.

"We could shout," Melissa said. "Or wait until he . . . Jed."

Walking up the steps from the corridor was a man in a blue uniform like the one the upstairs guard wore.

And behind him, head bowed, was Rhiannon.

Jed flattened himself against the wall, pulling Melissa with him. The guard led Rhiannon to the desk and handed her a pen; she bent down, writing, and Jed pulled Melissa quickly up the stairs and, under the astonished eyes of the lobby guard, outside. "There's no time for bikes," Jed gasped, leading Melissa around one side of the building—and as if he'd predicted it, Rhiannon came down the steps when they had only just managed to duck out of sight.

They watched her turn left at the bottom of the steps and walk slowly away along the sidewalk.

"I don't see why we couldn't just have gone right up to her," Melissa said when Rhiannon was out of sight. "Why couldn't we just have asked? I think we should, anyway, Jed. I mean we're just *guessing* she was seeing the hermit."

"We're going back," he said grimly. "I just didn't want her to know we're on to her."

"You make it sound as if she's doing something wrong," Melissa said angrily. "Suppose it's someone else she was seeing?"

"Well, we'll soon know if it is," he said.

They went back into the building, again managing to avoid the lobby guard, and down the stairs to the basement.

"Eli John Dunn?" The jail guard, who spoke very slowly, as if he had to think carefully to find each word, answered them through the grillwork. "Yes, we have a prisoner by that name. Had him a while, too. Goes to trial soon, though, for that kidnapping down to Fours Crossing. You heard about that, I'll wager. 'Twas in all the papers."

Melissa's knees felt weak again at mention of the trial, worse than they'd felt when she'd gotten off Gran's bike.

"Why?" asked the guard, peering at them shortsightedly. "You relatives or something? I dunno as I can let kids in to see him, 'specially given what he's done—what he's *accused* of doing, I should say. Have to ask the boss . . ."

"Oh, we don't want to see him," said Jed; Melissa could feel him shudder slightly next to her. "We were just wondering if—if he's been having any other—any visitors."

"Why, yes," the guard said. "His lawyer, of course, Mr. O'Callahan. And a lady, too, lately. Matter of fact, she just left. Name of—of . . ." He consulted the register. "Funny first name, don't know as I can say it."

"Rhiannon," Melissa heard herself supplying. "Jones."

"That's it," said the guard. "Rhia—what you said—Jones. Should I ask?" he said. "About you seeing the old man?"

"No," said Jed. "No, thank you."

"Thanks, anyway," Melissa called over her shoulder as they left.

They biked directly home, making no side trips, and were greeted by Gran, worried, gingerly holding out an official-looking paper, as if it were hot. "Chief Dupres was just here," she said, her face seeming older, the lines in it carved deeper, "with that summons Mr. Davis said you'd be getting, Melissa. You'll be getting one, too, Jed, and maybe Tommy. They've set a trial date— Oh, Melissa . . ." Gran put her arms around Melissa for a moment, terrifying her; Gran was always strong, stronger than anyone Melissa had ever known.

But Gran soon rallied. "I'm being foolish," she said, holding Melissa by the shoulders, pushing her back and smiling. "We should be glad, not sorry, because it'll soon be over and we can put that terrible time behind us, where it belongs." She put the summons carefully on the kitchen table, after holding it out to Melissa, who shook her head. "There's nothing to worry about," Gran said, with a somewhat forced smile.

"After all, that nice Mr. Davis went over his questions so carefully with you—and I called Mr. Savage, Melissa, and he said again that he'll stop in when he can between his own cases just to be with us and answer questions. And we'll call Daddy tonight—I expect he'll be getting one of these, too." She nodded toward the summons, looking as if she didn't want to touch it again. "Over soon, that's what we've got to concentrate on," she said, "hard as it'll be to relive it all and to see Eli John."

Melissa's stomach turned over once more, but she reached out and squeezed Gran's hand. "It's all right, Gran," she said, avoiding Jed's eyes. "After all, he can't get at us now."

"He'll be guarded, Miz Dunn. There's no need to worry." But Jed's smile, like Gran's, was a little forced. "It'll be fun, I bet," he said unenthusiastically, "being in court. Like the movies. KIDS TESTIFY AGAINST KIDNAPPER. I bet we even have our names in the paper again."

Now Melissa felt herself shudder.

9

That night, Melissa had an odd dream, in which she relived being forced by the hermit to march blindfolded through the snow to the root cellar, which he'd called a temple, where he'd kept her prisoner with Jed. That scene melted away almost as soon as it began, giving way to one in which the hermit, in a snow-white robe belted with gold, held the stolen spring plate above his head. As he lifted it, he began slowly circling the tripod he had set up in the middle of the root cellar–temple, and chanting the strange, foreign-sounding words that seemed to make the wind blow cold and the sky turn dark. But that scene faded, too, again almost instantly, to Spring Festival day, when everyone in Fours Crossing, led by the youngest schoolchild, little Susie Coffin, marched from Gran's to each house in the village and back again, singing a song that had seemed to bring spring for as many years as anyone could remember—till this year. This year the snow had not stopped falling from the cold and wintery sky until May, when the spring plate was finally safely back at Gran's . . .

The scene moved abruptly to inside Gran's house, again on

Spring Festival day, when Melissa and Jed had worked for hours to decipher the letters on the plates; that was when they'd realized that the plate the hermit had stolen was the one that said SPRINGE. Then Melissa saw herself alone in her room, deciphering the fragment of the old diary that had come apart in her hands, discovering it had been kept by Eben Dunn, the original hermit's son, back in 1725, the year the original hermit had died—or disappeared . . .

"Melissa? Melissa?"

It was Gran's voice, and Gran shaking her.

"Land, child, you've been making such a racket in your sleep! Are you all right?" Gran switched on the electrified kerosene lamp by Melissa's bed, and Melissa rubbed her eyes, confused. "What time is it?" she asked.

"Past three. Was it a dream, lambie?"

Melissa nodded.

"Want to tell me?"

"No," Melissa said. "It—it's all right, Gran. I'm sorry I woke you."

"It's that trial," Gran sighed. "I think it's terrible, putting you children through all that again. I do wish there were some way to avoid it." Gran smoothed Melissa's hair. "Let me get you some warm milk, lambie, that'll get you off to sleep again." She patted Melissa's hand and bustled away.

Gran had sounded angry. But it isn't the trial that's making me dream, Melissa thought, waiting for the milk; at least I don't think it is. It's something else . . .

She got out of bed and went to her window—and yes, as he often had done before the hermit was in jail, Ulfin was lying protectively outside. Melissa opened the window, and Ulfin looked gravely up at her, his tail brushing slowly against the newly green grass, but his ears alert, cocked toward the woods.

"Ulfin," Melissa whispered. "I'm glad you're here."

She went back to bed, and was already asleep when Gran came up with the milk. Her dreams began comfortably this time, but strangely—it was as if she were in the bottom of a deep, primeval valley, surrounded by mountains wider but not taller than Fours Crossing's, and greener, far greener but at the same time dark. She heard music—a harp not unlike Rhiannon's, and a sweet, clear voice—Rhiannon's, too?—singing foreign words. The music faded and then surged back again, this time as if sung by many voices in chorus.

Suddenly, just as Melissa felt lulled by the sound, there was silence and the valley vanished. Then came a high, cackling laugh—like—like the hermit's, Melissa realized, waking with a jolt and finding herself bathed in sweat.

She slept no more that night.

Sunday afternoon, Tommy suggested to Melissa that they go up to Rhiannon's again. "Let's just *ask* her what's going on in Hiltonville," he said. "Jed's—well, I know he says he's studying, but he's getting that look again, Melissa. You know, when he's inside himself instead of, well, with us."

Melissa, remembering Tommy's confiding in her once that he had a dream of running away with Jed and joining the Mounties, realized that Tommy was lonely for Jed as much as he was worried—but then so am I, she thought, lonely and worried both; Jed had barely smiled at her that morning outside church.

"Okay," she said aloud. "Let's go and see what we can find out."

It was hot as they climbed Round Top, and a summerlike haze hung low over the mountains. The air was heavy and still; bees and other insects were active and buzzing, but the birds seemed to have sought coolness deep within the woods.

"Feels like thunder," Tommy said when they reached the end of the fire road. Then he stopped abruptly.

From not far ahead came a gentle, clear strumming and Rhiannon's voice singing, Melissa realized with a start, the song that she had dreamed the night before.

Linnet ran out of the clearing to greet them, with Dian frisking behind; Tommy, laughing, went after Dian as she bounded to the brook. But Linnet ran up to Melissa and sat directly in front of her, much as Ulfin often did. Melissa, troubled, bent to pat her and then found herself kneeling, hugging the dog's warm, round body. "Linnet," she whispered, suddenly feeling unexplainably sad. "Linnet."

Linnet leaned against her, licking her face in short, quick laps, as if to reassure her.

"Welcome."

Rhiannon, in blue again, with her harp slung over her shoulder, stepped through the underbrush, smiling. She held out her hand to Melissa. "Are you all right?" she asked.

Melissa nodded, surprised; it was as if Rhiannon understood her sudden brief sadness.

But if so, Rhiannon gave no further sign. "Some tea?" she asked in an everyday voice. "Or lemonade—the heat."

"Oh, yes," Tommy said eagerly, coming back, cuddling Dian. "Lemonade would be super!"

They followed Rhiannon into her small clearing and helped her take a large jug of lemonade from the brook. It was ice-cold and wonderful—much better than tea would have been.

"I go to see the old hermit," said Rhiannon without preamble and without their asking, when they'd each finished one glass of lemonade and were starting on a second, "because he is my relative. I told you I came because of a relative. I did not tell you who for fear of alarming you."

Tommy put his lemonade down, wide-eyed. "Your *relative?*"

he said. "But he's Melissa's relative, too, distantly. You must be related to her!"

Rhiannon smiled at Melissa. "I am," she said. "But then, we are all related, Tommy, far enough back."

"You and me?" said Tommy, looking mystified. "Melissa and me? *Jed* and me?" He laughed. "I'd like that," he said ingenuously, "but it's not possible. We'd know if we were related. Why, here in Fours Crossing . . ."

"Anything," said Rhiannon, stroking Linnet, "is possible."

"They've sent for us to testify at the trial," Melissa told Rhiannon, curling her feet under her on the brook's bank, where they were sitting. "If he's your relative—well, maybe you'll mind that."

Rhiannon shook her head. "He has broken many laws," she said softly, "and he must accept punishment." She looked away from them sadly. "He will not, though," she said. "Nothing I say brings him round."

"You mean," said Melissa, trying to work it out, "that you came here to try to make him—well, repent, sort of?"

"Something like that," Rhiannon said. "But"—she spread her hands in a gesture almost of dismissal—"but he is too stubborn, too twisted and warped. More twisted and warped by far," she said, "than that which he has tried zealously but foolishly to combat."

Linnet, with a glance at Rhiannon, went to Melissa and, sighing, snuggled next to her, her head on Melissa's lap.

Melissa felt taken back to the time in the root cellar when the hermit had talked to them about what he called the Old Ways and accused Fours Crossing of corrupting them by enacting the Spring Festival ritual with—what had he said? —"frivolity instead of deep and solemn joy"? Something like that.

"You mean the Old Ways and the New Ways?" Melissa

asked, while Tommy looked more mystified than ever but remained silent.

Rhiannon nodded. "Yes," she said gently. "The hermit clings to the Old Ways of worshipping and of living. The village clings increasingly to the New. There is no way between—no door—unless . . ." She smiled at both Melissa and Linnet. "Unless someone is willing to open it, and someone is willing to walk through, leading the others, joining Old and New. For without that, there can be no future. Listen." She picked up her harp and began strumming again, softly, the melody from Melissa's dream. Dian, as if drawn by the music, walked to them and stood between Rhiannon and the two children. As the music grew more complex, Dian shook her head, flicking ears and tail; then, as Rhiannon sang foreign words again, weaving her song around the melody she played on her harp, Dian ran away to the field beyond the brook. Linnet raised her head from Melissa's lap, but did not follow.

Melissa felt chilled despite the now-oppressive heat, and hugged Linnet closer; Tommy, she noticed, had moved closer to Rhiannon. The big white clouds in the sky had turned gray and heavy, pressing down on them, much nearer to them on Round Top, it seemed, than they would have been in the village. Thunder rolled steadily now, like an oncoming herd.

"No future?" Melissa whispered, feeling a desperate sadness when the song was over.

"No true one," Rhiannon said, "without the joining."

"But how does the joining happen?" Melissa asked her. "How?"

Rhiannon only smiled at her and sang again.

Halfway through the song, there was a frantic rustling in the woods and Jed, pale and breathless, burst through, preceded by Ulfin. Ulfin ran straight to Linnet and touched noses with her; she jumped to her feet and stood trembling, watching him—and Jed faced Melissa and Tommy. "The trial," he panted, out of breath from running, "the trial starts tomorrow. They moved it up—he's been acting strange, they said, the old hermit, I mean . . ." He looked at Rhiannon now, accusingly.

"She's on our side, Jed," Melissa said. "She's been trying to help, to talk to him, to . . ."

But the rain came then, chasing them all inside the cottage.

10

The newspapers rushed extra editions into print: KIDNAP-PING TRIAL STARTS TODAY, one said the next morning, and that evening, JURY SELECTED IN KIDNAPPING TRIAL. ACCUSED TO FACE VICTIMS, blared one paper the next day, which was the day actual arguments were to start and Jed and Melissa were to appear; CHILD VICTIMS IN COURT, shouted another. Melissa tried to ignore them, but it was hard; newspaper vendors lined the sidewalks in Hiltonville when she, Tommy, and Jed, who had been excused from school, drove up with Gran in Mr. Savage's car. Melissa's father, who was going to have to testify, too, was meeting them in court after driving all night from Washington.

The courtroom itself was thronged. It was as if the whole village of Fours Crossing had come for the trial, and most of Hiltonville besides. The room wasn't big enough to hold them all, so many people had to be turned away—but not before those who didn't know them had peered and pointed at Jed and Melissa.

"It's awful," Melissa whispered to Jed and Tommy as, with Gran, they joined Rhiannon and Seth on one of the hard, pewlike benches lined up in neat rows in the stuffy, oak-paneled courtroom—Stanley wasn't there yet. Seth, in what appeared to be a new sports jacket, looked tense but hangover-free. Rhiannon was pale and still; Jed, Melissa saw, wouldn't look at either Rhiannon or Seth.

"Cheer up, you two," Tommy whispered a little anxiously as some people in front of Jed and Melissa looked their way and whispered. "How bad can it be to be famous?"

"Well, *I* hate it," Melissa said. She could see from the embarrassment on Jed's face that he hated it, too.

Just then there was a bustle in one of the aisles, and Melissa's father came hurrying toward them, looking haggard from his long drive. He slipped onto the bench where Melissa was, between her and Jed. "Okay, pigeon?" he asked, kissing her quickly, and she nodded, relieved beyond words that he was there.

Right after that, the jury filed in—eight men and four women, all very solemn—and a moment later a thick silence fell on the courtroom as a small door opened toward the front and the hermit himself was led into a separate booth with waist-high wooden walls, called, Mr. Savage had explained on the way to court, the dock, where prisoners had to sit during their trials. The hermit was handcuffed; he shuffled into the dock between two guards, head bowed, with no trace of his former fire. His clothes looked shapeless, too big—but then Melissa realized she had never seen him in proper clothes. She'd seen him only in the black robe he wore for everyday, and the special snow-white ceremonial one he had used when he held up the spring plate and chanted.

The door clicked shut behind the hermit and he sat down, his head still bowed, his wispy white hair grown so long that it fell over his shoulders and lost itself in the white of his long beard. He looked beaten, almost humble.

"Holy cow," Jed said softly, and Seth put his hand on Jed's shoulder for a moment.

"Poor old thing," Gran breathed, with a brief sympathetic shake of her head. "He's lost weight."

Stanley Dunn moved closer to Melissa. "Steady," he whispered.

At the same moment the hermit raised his head and turned his black eyes full on Melissa and Jed, finding them instantly; had someone told him where they would be sitting? Melissa felt her bones turn to water under his piercing stare, and she reached for her father's hand. The hermit's face was defiant, rather than defeated, and the coldness of his eyes fell on both Melissa and Jed like a sudden arctic wind. Melissa had to remind herself that she was in a courtroom, with Daddy, Chief Dupres and Charley, and other friendly people all around her, instead of trapped with Jed in the cold and lonely root cellar.

Just as Melissa thought she could no longer bear the hermit's eyes on her, he shifted his gaze to Rhiannon, inclining his head toward her. She returned his nod, ever so slightly, her face as expressionless as his.

"All rise!" A sigh swept through the courtroom, as if everyone had been holding their breath since the hermit's entrance, and there was a shuffling and a scraping as everyone stood up. Another door opened, this one behind the slightly raised platform at the front of the room, and a stately gray-haired woman with a stern but kindly face glided in, black robes billowing around her. For a moment she stood still, surveying the crowded room; then she nodded slightly and sat down.

Mr. Savage, who had explained that he had a case in another courtroom in the same building and so would be in and out, slipped onto the bench behind Melissa and Jed and leaned over, with difficulty, for he was plump like his daughter. Also like her, though, he had an air of down-to-earth capability that was very reassuring. "That's the judge," he said, gesturing toward the black-robed woman. "Judge Cabot. Now," he went on, whispering as Judge Cabot began going through some papers with her clerk, a small thin man with a face like a sparrow's, "the first one to speak will be Mr. Davis, whom you already know." Mr. Savage nodded toward a table just below the judge's platform where two men were talking animatedly. One was white-haired, ruddy-faced Mr. Davis, who looked if anything a bit more florid than usual, and the other, as if in purposeful contrast to him, was a very pale man, round-shouldered, though tall. Much to Melissa's surprise, he didn't look much older than she imagined Jed might look in a year or two. "That fellow," said Mr. Savage, indicating the pale man, "the tall young one who looks as if he's never been out-doors even to mow his front lawn, is Mr. O'Callahan, the defense attorney. That means he's the hermit's lawyer. He'll be asking you questions, too, as Mr. Davis has no doubt told you. And, as I said, the judge is Judge Cabot. She's tough, but usually very fair."

"Tough enough to put the old bird away for good, I hope," Seth muttered with a glance at Jed, and Tommy nodded— but Jed bent down as if to tie his shoe. Poor Mr. Ellison, Melissa thought; he's trying so hard. Then she saw Rhiannon cover Seth's hand for a second with her own.

"Good luck," Mr. Savage whispered. "I'll be back later."

And then the trial began in earnest.

There were a lot of big words, and a lot of complicated sentences Melissa couldn't follow, and Jed and Tommy looked so puzzled Melissa was sure they couldn't, either. The jurors listened intently, though, and most of them looked as if they understood, as did Gran and Melissa's and Jed's fathers. "A heinous crime," Mr. Davis called the kidnapping, shouting his opening statement even more loudly than he'd shouted in Gran's kitchen, "leading two poor terrified children through the woods in deep snow . . . put in terror of their lives . . . the state will show . . . and the state will prove . . . assault and battery as well . . . larceny . . . diabolical . . . terrible, terrible crime . . ."

The hermit sat impassively during Mr. Davis's opening statement, but when his own lawyer, pale Mr. O'Callahan, slowly stood up, he leaned forward and fixed him with his piercing stare. Mr. O'Callahan, Melissa thought, looked uncomfortable, perhaps partly because of his round-shouldered stoop—and he certainly seemed to be avoiding looking at the hermit, even though he was talking about him, trying to explain him to the jurors. "Mr. Dunn has served the village of Fours Crossing faithfully and loyally for years," Mr. O'Callahan said mournfully, his voice sounding as if it were coming through a tunnel, "as Forest Keeper—a lonely job, when taken literally as he seems to have taken it. The defendant is a lonely old man, nearing the end of his days . . ." Here the hermit stiffened and seemed about to speak, but his guards stepped forward and he closed his mouth. ". . . no actual physical harm done the children . . . somewhat deluded, it is true . . . *not guilty by reason of insanity*."

At those words the hermit sprang to his feet, shrieking, and pointed a gnarled and claw-like finger at Mr. O'Callahan. "Traitor!" he shouted in his reedy but strong voice; Melissa cringed to hear it again. Then she fought against her fear and forced herself to look straight at him. "I warned you! You persist in vilifying me! It is *they* who are deluded . . ." His hand swept the courtroom in a gesture that included everyone present. ". . . they who are . . ."

"Order!" the judge said sternly, rapping for attention with

a wooden gavel. "Mr. O'Callahan, will you please approach the bench? Guards, kindly restrain the prisoner."

"It is the village, the village that is ill," the hermit cried as his guards laid hold of him, forcing him to sit, "with a great sickness."

The judge rose and the uniformed court officers—a little like policemen—who had until now been standing around the edges of the room looking bored, moved in toward the dock. But before they got there, Rhiannon, with a rustle of her blue cloak, rose and faced the hermit sternly. "Eli son of Eli," she said, her voice ringing out over the astonished spectators—Seth, seeming embarrassed, glanced anxiously at Jed, who looked away—"Eli John Dunn, last of the direct line, be seated and be silent! You are being given fair trial by these people, carefully and rightly according to their laws. It is acceptable, as I have told you. You must . . ."

For a moment the court officers stood as if paralyzed, but now some of them began to move toward Rhiannon, others toward the hermit. Judge Cabot pounded her gavel again. "Clear the court," she commanded. "Yes, remove that woman first."

"Your honor," said Rhiannon calmly, "I can quiet him. Look."

All eyes turned toward the hermit, who had sunk to his seat again and was hunched there, head bowed and silent.

Whispers rustled through the courtroom. Tommy, on one side of Melissa, seemed to be holding his breath.

"Let me speak to him further," said Rhiannon. "Let me explain to him. I am," she went on, "a distant relative."

Judge Cabot put her hand briefly to her head; her mouth was a thin, tense line. "This court must be cleared. The jurors are excused. Mr. Davis, Mr. O'Callahan, kindly approach the bench. Court officers . . ."

The court officers opened the doors and ushered everyone out.

DISTURBANCE IN COURT, the newspaper headlines shouted that night. STRANGE WOMAN CALMS DEFENDANT. COURT ORDERED CLEARED.

"Tune in tomorrow," Jed said disgustedly into his beef stew; he was having dinner with Gran, Melissa, and Melissa's father, having grumpily turned down Seth and Rhiannon's invitation to eat with them in Hiltonville—and it was just as well, Melissa had thought on the way home, that Rhiannon and Seth didn't come along too, for on the way they passed a group of children giggling and chanting "Witchy, witchy, witchy" again.

"If you ask me," Jed said, "that Rhiannon's being more trouble than help."

Melissa glanced at Gran in desperation. "But she *did* help, Jed, couldn't you see? Gran, didn't she help?"

"It certainly seemed so," Gran said cautiously, moving the newspaper aside and passing the bread. "She seemed to want to. I wonder if she's talked to Seth, though, about whatever it is she's doing. It does look odd—and it must trouble Seth— still, perhaps she has good reason . . ."

"Dad says she hasn't said anything to him," said Jed. "At least he says she hasn't said much, whatever that means. You'd think she'd talk to him if they're so"—he threw his fork down and pushed back his chair—"so tangled up with each other. Except how someone like Dad could believe in—oh, who knows? Excuse me." He slammed out of the kitchen.

Melissa followed him into the dining room, where he was standing in front of the plates, his hands thrust deep into his pockets, frowning.

"Jed," she said, "I know it seems wrong—Rhiannon knowing the hermit so well and all, when he did what he did to us. But—well, remember how Rhiannon showed me the summer plate? It's as if something's *brewing*, almost, and she's trying to stop it. I don't know, maybe she hasn't said anything to your dad because she thinks he might not understand— come on, you know he wouldn't! Look at how long it took us to understand the—the power the hermit has. I'm not sure we really understand it even now, but, Jed, if anyone's trying to help, it's Rhiannon. I'm sure of that!" Am I, she wondered, less certain than she sounded. But I have to be . . .

Jed laughed sardonically. "Good old Melissa," he said nastily. "You've sure come a long way since March, when you didn't believe anything except what could be proved scientifically. Sure, I remember about the summer plate. But the trouble is," he said, turning to face her, "how can we really know whose side she's on? And what power *she* has?"

"I don't know," Melissa said, less certain still, and hurt. She thought uncomfortably of Rhiannon's song, and of the deep green valley she'd seen in her dream, but then she remembered what Rhiannon had said about the joining and about there being a door between. "I think it's you who doesn't believe this time," she said finally, sure again. "I really do, Jed. I'm pretty sure I trust Rhiannon. I don't understand what's happening, but I think you should try to trust her, too."

But Jed shook his head silently, and went home without finishing his dinner. And the next morning, during Gran's brief testimony about the stolen plate, and later while both their fathers described finding Jed and Melissa in the woods, Jed was withdrawn, and silent, and unreadable. He didn't smile along with everyone else when Tommy, telling about his part in the rescue, said in a loud, clear voice, "Well, okay, I was the first *human* there, but Ulfin was the one who really found them"—and he sat motionless, not reacting at all, when

Chief Dupres described the hidden root cellar and, later, his arrest of the hermit.

Right before lunchtime, Mr. O'Callahan surprised everyone by deciding not to cross-examine Charley, who was Mr. Davis's last witness—and before she really knew what was happening, Melissa herself was on the witness stand, looking out over what seemed to be a roomful of strangers—sympathetic strangers, but strangers nonetheless. She could feel the hermit's eyes on her, even though she didn't dare even glance his way. She looked at her father instead, and Gran, but even though they both smiled and nodded reassuringly, her mouth was dry and her hand shook when she held it up and swore to tell the truth. How could she promise that when she knew the truth was so improbable she barely believed it herself?

The first questions were easy: her name, and where she lived, and how long she'd lived there, and what grade she was in—things like that. Then came questions about the plate's being stolen and about how she and Jed had decided to try to get it back. It was easy enough to talk about that without saying too much about the plate's power; easy to point out that the Spring Festival procession had always started and ended at Gran's house, outside her dining-room window, in full view of the wall where the plates hung. No one asked anything about why, and Melissa was just as glad Mr. Davis had warned her not to volunteer information that wasn't asked for.

But then the questions got harder. Melissa, conscious of Rhiannon's eyes on her, and Jed's, and most of all the hermit's, began to falter when Mr. Davis asked, "Did the hermit talk to you about the plate?"

"Yes," she said softly, dreading what she knew was coming next, for she was sure no one would believe it.

"What did he say about the plate?"

"He—well, he told us that it—brought spring," she answered carefully, "and—well, that he was keeping it so spring wouldn't come, because he was angry at the village for—well, he thought the village was doing the Festival wrong . . ."

Out of the corner of her eye, to her horror, Melissa saw the hermit smiling.

". . . and—and . . ." she faltered.

"That is right, Tabitha," the hermit cried, leaping to his feet, his baggy clothes flapping around him. "Good girl; well done; you are a true priestess, after all! True wife to my son! Now they will see!"

"Order!" Judge Cabot shouted, pounding her gavel; the jurors looked confused. "Restrain the defendant!"

Then Mr. O'Callahan started asking questions, and Melissa had to explain that the hermit had always called her Tabitha and Jed, Eben, after the first Eli Dunn's son and daughter-in-law, with whom he seemed to confuse them.

At last they broke for lunch, but Melissa found she couldn't eat, even though her father kept saying how proud he was of her. Jed, she noticed, ate very little also, and spoke even less; it was going to be his turn to testify first thing that afternoon. "Good luck," she whispered to him when they were back in court and the clerk had called him. Seth smiled at him and said, "You'll do fine, lad. Just speak up clearly, that's all."

Jed gave them both an absent smile.

He did do fine, although as the questions got harder he began to seem uncomfortable, as Melissa had herself. Finally the judge said, "This is unorthodox, but I think if both lawyers will agree, we will be able to sort this story out better if we allow this young man to explain in his own words what happened." The lawyers looked displeased, but they both nodded.

"Well," said Jed, "I—I'm not sure I can, but . . ." He turned to the judge. "I have to just say what everyone did, don't I, not what I thought about it, or what Melissa thought about it?"

For the first time so far in the trial, Judge Cabot smiled. "Let's say you should try to do that," she told him. "I'll let you know if you start interpreting too much."

Jed took a deep breath. "Well," he began, "as Melissa said, when he had us there in the temp—in the root cellar that he called a temple, he kept calling me Eben and Melissa, Tabitha, after people who lived centuries ago, back in the 1700s. And so . . ."

"Your honor," said Mr. Davis, standing up, his face very red, "all this is most interesting from a historical standpoint, but I really don't see . . ."

Judge Cabot waved him aside. "Go on, Jethro," she said.

Jed cleared his throat. "Well," he said, "Melissa's gran had told us that the first Eli Dunn, back in seventeen-something, had been mad at the village because Bradford Ellison—that's the one there's a statue of in Fours Crossing—had come up from Boston to start a church. There hadn't ever been a church there before. The idea of having a church made old Eli Dunn angry, only no one seems to have known why. Then when his son Eben up and married Bradford Ellison's daughter Tabitha, he got so mad he went out into the woods and built a house—the Keeper's House, the one the hermit lives in—and he never went back to the village again. And I guess he went kind of crazy out there, only no one knows what really happened to him in the end—how he died, I mean, because . . ."

Melissa sensed rather than saw the guards move closer to the hermit, who was shifting restlessly around in his seat.

". . . because there aren't any town records for the year he was last seen in, 1725. But anyway, we—this is interpreta-

96

tion, I guess," Jed interrupted himself, turning to the judge. "Is it okay?"

Mr. O'Callahan had been nodding, a pleased half-smile on his pale face, but Mr. Davis, whose face was shiny now as well as red, looked as if he was about to jump to his feet. Judge Cabot, her mouth twitching, said, "Go ahead."

"Well, we—Melissa and I—we sort of thought that he—our hermit, Eli John Dunn—thought that he was the *first* Eli Dunn, or was pretending to be or something like that, because he was sort of acting out the story of the first Eli and he was doing all those ceremonies and stuff that Melissa told about, and saying that Spring Festival was all wrong the way we did it . . ."

"It was wrong!" the hermit shouted. "It is!"

Rhiannon, with a glance at the judge, glared at the hermit, and he fell silent.

"Mr. Davis," said the judge, just when Melissa thought Mr. Davis was on the point of exploding, "do you have any questions at this point?"

"Indeed I do, your honor," said Mr. Davis. He strode rapidly to the witness box and, turning partway toward the jury, said in his loud voice, "Now, Jethro, isn't it true that the hermit held you against your will—forced you to stay with him?"

"Yes, sir," said Jed.

Mr. Davis smiled slightly and sat down.

"Mr. O'Callahan?" said Judge Cabot.

Mr. O'Callahan got unhurriedly to his feet and smiled faintly at Jed. "Did the hermit say in what way he felt that Spring Festival as Fours Crossing celebrated it was wrong?" he asked.

"Your honor," said Mr. Davis, his voice taut, "may I respectfully remind my brother counsel, Mr. O'Callahan, that we are trying a kidnapping case here, not Spring Festival as celebrated in the village of Fours Crossing? I'm afraid I fail to see the relevance of this."

At that, there was a titter in the courtroom, and the questions were resumed—facts again, about whether the hermit had hurt them physically (he'd shaken them a few times, and pulled Melissa's hair—bad enough—and he'd nearly killed Ulfin—but even so, no one could say he'd done any lasting physical harm to any of them).

"Well," said Gran when it was over and they were leaving for the day, "I think you did splendidly, both of you."

But Melissa wasn't so sure. She'd been trying when she could to listen as a juror might, and she had to admit that if she were a juror she'd find the whole story as hard to believe as she'd found Spring Festival and the plate's power when she'd first come to Fours Crossing. It was as if there were a little bit of magic—something not quite real, anyway—in the middle of a very real place and among very real people. And who, in the twentieth century, could possibly accept that? Still, if it made the jurors think the hermit was crazy—well, then maybe it was all right.

The next day it was Mr. O'Callahan's turn to present his defense. He asked the judge's permission to call Jed again, and then Melissa, asking them both about the foreign-sounding words the hermit had chanted during his "ceremonies" with the plate—words that, Melissa testified, were real words backward. "The right way around," she said, "they're the words to a song like the one everyone sings at Spring Festival. The first line, 'Eb dedne dloc sretniw,' means 'Winter's cold ended be.' "

Melissa heard a surprised murmur as the spectators turned to each other, whispering.

"No further questions," said Mr. O'Callahan, and Melissa went uneasily back to her seat.

"I would like to point out," said Mr. O'Callahan elegantly, leaning toward the jury, "if the court will permit, that according to ancient folklore"—he waved a book—"saying a good thing, a prayer, for example, backwards is supposed to constitute a spell, often an evil one. I will call experts to testify to that. And I submit that this—spell—shows my client's mind was so pitifully deranged when he took the children that he actually believed that this backwards song and all his ceremonies were responsible for last winter's persistence well into May, and furthermore . . ."

"Mr. O'Callahan," said the judge dryly, "I was not aware you were a witness in this case. And you will have ample time for a summation later. For now, let us hear from your folklore expert."

A Professor Gidgins was called, and after him a Professor Cantnor, both of whom backed up what Mr. O'Callahan had said about spells. And then came Dr. Foster and Dr. Hughes, both psychiatrists. Each of them testified that he had examined the hermit and found him "competent to stand trial," but otherwise mentally ill, because, among other things, he still believed he had the power to prevent spring from coming.

And then it was over for that day.

"There is danger," Rhiannon said with a troubled sigh as they left the courtroom, "in experts who are not experts. Great danger." She turned away then, following Seth.

Jed looked at Melissa. "What did she mean by that?" he asked.

"I'm not sure," Melissa said uncomfortably.

The next day the weather turned suddenly hot—"like August," said Gran, "even though it's only the second of June," and everyone in the courtroom grew increasingly bedraggled and short-tempered as the day progressed. It was Rhiannon who was stared at now, more than Jed and Melissa; her name had been in the paper again that morning. "Look at the words they use," Jed said indignantly before Judge Cabot came in. "Says the hermit has 'deadly eyes,' and that Rhiannon 'stares him down like a gypsy putting the evil eye on someone.'"

Melissa smiled, and was about to point out that Jed was coming very close to actually defending Rhiannon, when Mr. Savage bustled in and sat behind them. "Good news," he said. "It looks as if you won't miss your exams or even much more school. Closing arguments will probably be today. Mr. Davis has a few more witnesses he thinks might show the hermit is sane after all, but that should just about finish things up." He smiled at them, but then added more seriously, "After the closing arguments, the jury'll go out and decide if the hermit's guilty or not guilty—of each charge; remember, there are two: stealing the plate and kidnapping you."

"Which way will it go?" Jed asked uncomfortably.

"It's hard to say, Jed," Mr. Savage answered, blotting his perspiring forehead with a folded handkerchief. "I suppose he'll probably be found guilty of stealing the plate. As for the kidnapping—well, ordinarily, people are pretty hard on kidnappers. But I think Mr. O'Callahan's going to keep hammering away at the hermit's age—if you can say Mr. O'Callahan hammers away at anything—and the fact that he didn't actually hurt you—really seriously, I mean."

"Could—could he get free altogether?" Melissa asked anxiously.

Mr. Savage hesitated just long enough for Melissa to feel nervous. Then he patted her hand and said, "It's not likely. He'll be going either to jail or to a mental hospital, I'm pretty sure." He gripped their shoulders. "Which means it'll be over soon, you two. You've been great, you know. You've done Fours Crossing proud."

The closing arguments were very much as Mr. Savage had said they would be. First Mr. O'Callahan got up and calmly but forcefully said a lot of flowery things about the hermit's being a poor old man so isolated from the community that he'd become mentally ill. That his "natural interest" in history and in the customs of Fours Crossing and in his own ancestry had led him "to a morbid obsession" that had "snapped his mind." Anyone who could believe in "pagan powers that do not exist," Mr. O'Callahan finished, was "obviously a sad victim of insanity."

"Look at Rhiannon," Melissa whispered to Jed, startled.

Rhiannon was staring at Mr. O'Callahan with a look of such combined pity and alarm that neither Jed nor Melissa could take their eyes off her. Imperceptibly, as Mr. O'Callahan sat down, her lips moved. "*Fool*," Melissa thought she heard in the faintest of whispers.

The hermit himself looked furious. He twitched and muttered, but as if he'd learned his lesson earlier, he kept to his seat and said nothing that anyone could hear.

Melissa's father put his arm around her.

Then Mr. Davis got up, mopping at his face with a handkerchief. "Despite all that my brother counsel, Mr. O'Callahan, has said, we cannot forget the seriousness of the crime"— his voice rose—"and the fear that these children"—he gestured toward them—"suffered, the ordeal that they and their families were put through. If the children hadn't been found by the police—" Here his voice fell dramatically. Chief Dupres and Charley sat up very straight, but Tommy, who had again been allowed to skip school for the day, looked indignant. After all, it had been he and Ulfin, not the police, who had actually found Jed and Melissa. "—rescued by the police," Mr. Davis was saying, "they might still be in this man's remote—er—cave today, being used for the good Lord only knows what nefarious purpose. Yes, Mr. Dunn may be an old man, yes, he may have mental problems—but let us not in our compassion for him forget to have compassion for his victims or—one trembles to think of it—his possible future victims." His voice was rising to a crescendo and he punctuated his final words with jabs of his hand toward the jury. "Let us not, ladies and gentlemen, forget the terrible crime that even the defense does not deny took place."

11

Judge Cabot then talked to the jury, giving them complicated instructions that Melissa could barely follow, full of
terms like "reasonable doubt" and "criminally responsible."
Then the judge sent the jury out of the courtroom to reach
their decision, and Jed and Melissa spent the rest of that long,
muggy afternoon trying to study in a little office Mr. Davis
used when he was in court.

Finally, the jury sent word that they were as far from a
decision as when they'd started—so court was adjourned till
Monday, and everyone went home except the jury, who had
to spend the weekend in the Hiltonville Arms Hotel, away
from newspapers and TV sets and other people so they
wouldn't be influenced by anyone.

To Melissa and Jed, time seemed suspended that weekend;
studying was next to impossible, and so was pretty much
everything else. The weather didn't make things any easier.
The valley in which Fours Crossing was nestled lay wrapped
in dry, hazy heat. It had rained very little since the flood and
newly sprouted crops began drooping; the very earth seemed
to shrivel, consuming itself for lack of moisture. "All that

rain," Gran sighed, watering her vegetable patch sparingly, in order not to deplete her well. "It's as if it never happened. I can't think where the rainwater's all gone!"

Rhiannon said nothing, but she looked worried when Melissa saw her on Saturday morning, and, Melissa noticed in the village at noontime, the whispers about her seemed to grow as the heat grew.

"For heaven's sake!" Miss Laurent exclaimed Saturday at the village baseball team's opening game—Tommy got two hits—when some of the seventh-graders started whispering about weather spells and Rhiannon. "You know what Mark Twain said about New England weather, don't you? If you don't like it, wait a few minutes and it'll change."

Several of the Sevens laughed, and Melissa's father said, "Right you are, Miss Laurent," but someone else said, "That's just the point, Miss Laurent: it isn't changing. As if there were a spell on it or something."

If there's a spell, thought Melissa, it's not of Rhiannon's making—but she couldn't very well say that out loud.

On Sunday, Mrs.-Ellison-the-librarian telephoned Melissa as she had promised and told her that the thin packet of pages Melissa had found in the desk had finally dried out enough to open. "Had it in the refrigerator," Mrs. Ellison said rather proudly over the phone, "and a good thing, in this weather." But she added that she was sorry to say that most of the print on the pages inside was illegible. There was only one short bit, she said, that anyone could possibly read; it didn't make much sense, but yes, of course, Melissa was welcome to come and see it; the library was open from one to five on Sundays.

When Melissa and Jed looked at it, it made a good deal more sense to them than it had to Mrs. Ellison.

. . . and the [word illegible] burned and crackled with great vehemence this Beltane of 1725, and there were those who said it was because it was so late. And we encased him in wicker, as of Old, and the wicker [illegible] and him with it and though his voice rose horribly saying, "I will return," his power could not arrest the [illegible]. Thus vanished forever the wicked false priest and his evil pagan ways, and all of Fours Crossing rejoiced and gave thanks unto the Lord.

" '. . . burned and crackled,' " Melissa said uncomfortably, not wanting to face what she was thinking as she copied the passage down. "That sounds . . ."

"Wicker," Jed interrupted, frowning. "Wait." He went past Mrs. Ellison, who was so busy working at her desk that she didn't look up, and flipped through a thick book from the folk-lore section. "Beltane," he said, returning to Melissa and paraphrasing what he read. "Common ancient festival in May. Usually May first. Mostly Celtic. Some tribes were rumored to enclose criminals in wicker and burn them—sacrifice them —to make fields fertile . . ." He let out a low whistle. "Holy cow," he said. "So that was it. No wonder they didn't list a cause of death. They—they killed him!" He looked at Melissa, horror on his face.

"If," said Melissa slowly, her voice sounding odd even to her, "they're talking about who we think they are—about the first Eli Dunn."

Jed went on as if he hadn't heard her. "A punishment," he said. "For old Eli's being against the church—like witch burning . . ."

They looked at each other then, the horror growing, thinking of the loaded words the papers had been using in their accounts of the trial, and about Rhiannon. *Witchy, witchy, witchy*, thought Melissa, feeling her whole body grow cold.

"And later," said Jed thickly, "maybe years later, some decent person might have been so—ashamed at what his town had done to old Eli that he tore this part of the book out and destroyed the records for 1725. A dark passage from the past that at least one person wanted to forget."

"Even if Bradford Ellison was the first minister in Fours Crossing," said Melissa, "he must have been a terrible hypocrite to use something pagan to punish someone for *being* pagan—if that's what the Old Ways were."

"Oh, they were pagan, all right," said Jed. "Look at all those sort of religious ceremonies the hermit did with the plate, and how the plates are marked with the names of the seasons and all. That's nature worship if I ever saw it. And Beltane— that was pagan. Look at all that stuff you deciphered in Eben Dunn's diary about the first Eli not liking it when Bradford Ellison came up here from Boston and started that church. Eli didn't like it because he was a pagan—and remember, he founded Fours Crossing, so other people here must have been pagans, too, at least until after the church came along. And if that Beltane stuff is right—well, it seems to me that Bradford Ellison just used the criminal's own laws to punish him with."

"But if being pagan is a religion," Melissa said angrily, "why punish anyone for it? And burning—that's barbaric, no matter who does it."

"Maybe that's the point," Jed said grimly, "sort of an eye for an eye—pagans were barbaric, after all, at least a lot of them were. And Christians were just as bad for a while, maybe worse, burning heretics, burning witches. Almost anyone can be barbaric, especially over religion, I guess." He put the folklore book back and looked hard at Melissa. "Even people who seem nice."

It haunted Melissa from then on, the idea of burning

witches, especially after she heard the children chanting their jump-rope rhyme again as she walked home. She made them stop, but she knew they would probably start up again as soon as she left.

On Monday morning, they all went back to Hiltonville, but the jury showed no sign of reaching a decision then either. Melissa's father had to go back to Washington that afternoon, so as soon as they got home, Gran made a stupendous goodbye picnic of deviled eggs, cold chicken, lemonade, and chocolate cake. She, Melissa, Stanley, and Jed ate it under an oak tree in the far corner of the field behind Gran's house, near the stone wall, while Ulfin snoozed and Pride and Joy chased butterflies in the sun. Then Stanley left, promising again to write and call but warning Melissa that he was going to have to start traveling in earnest soon, and would therefore be harder to reach.

After helping clean up the picnic things, Jed went home to study. "You might as well do some studying, too, lambie," Gran said. "Might as well go back to school tomorrow, also, if they don't reach a verdict. You've missed too much already —and besides, school will help keep your mind off the trial."

But the next day—another hot one—was only a half day at school because of some teachers' meetings. After lunch, Jed, yawning, grumbled that he'd been up till three a.m. waiting for his father to come home and that he was too sleepy and too hot to concentrate on his books. It didn't take much for Melissa to convince him to take a leisurely walk up Round Top with her to escape the heat in the village.

"Look," he said, stopping halfway up while Ulfin, still wet from a quick swim in the river, sniffed at a rabbit hole. Jed waved his arm in an arc that took in most of the valley.

Spread all around below them was green grass turning brown and plowed earth whitening into dust.

"Gran's peas all died," said Melissa.

Jed nodded. "Peas want it cool," he said, yawning again. "Like lettuce. Ground's hot enough for corn, but it'll grow weak in this drought; the ground's too dry to hold the roots." He shook his head. "I saw a couple of farmers planting yesterday all the same. Seems dumb." With a sudden smile he said, "I bet back in the pagan days that the first Eli liked so much, they'd have paid more attention to the weather and waited to start putting in their crops."

Ulfin's collar jingled as he scratched one ear. "I ought to get him a flea collar," Jed said, watching him. "Right, lad?"

Ulfin went on scratching, his head bobbing up and down as if he were agreeing.

"It'll look funny," said Melissa, trying to visualize a white or no-color plastic collar next to Ulfin's elegant three-stranded gold one.

"Umm," said Jed, stretching. He threw himself down on a log. "Can't we stay here?" he said, closing his eyes. "It's cool enough."

"You just don't want to see Rhiannon," Melissa said. "She's probably not even there, anyway. Come on—it's cooler near the brook. And"—she bent down to him, her face close to his —"she keeps lemonade in it. Cold as Gran's fridge."

Jed, grinning, got up.

Melissa turned out to be right about Rhiannon's not being there, although the kittens were curled up on the stone steps, and Dian was sleeping in her pen under a shelf that served as a shelter-plus-hayrack. Linnet, who was sprawled on her side under a tree, lifted her head when Ulfin went up to her, then wagged her tail and touched noses with him.

108

Melissa went to the door and knocked, but there was no answer.

"Looks as if there's a note or something on the table," said Jed, peering in through the window. Then he tried the door, pushed it open, and went in.

"Maybe the note's not for us, Jed," Melissa said, following him inside. "It's not likely to be since . . ." Then she saw his face and stopped. "What is it?"

He shook his head and stared down at the note, turning it over to read the back. Then without a word he handed it to Melissa and went outside.

Seth dear [Melissa read],

I thought it best I not be here when you came today. Last night was lovely, truly. But quite my mistake. As I told you, I am going to have to leave sometime soon; it would not be right for me to let you hope. I am so terribly sorry, Seth.

But remember that this means someday there could be, will be, someone else for you, not to take Bethany's place, but to keep you warm and to mother your wonderful boy, who you know cares deeply for you. Be gentle with Jed, and he will be gentle with you, I know it.

Forgive me, Seth.

Rhiannon

Jed was behind the cottage, near where the rescued animals had been before Rhiannon set them free. Only a few were left, among them the young sparrow hawk with his rapidly mending wing.

But Jed was clearly beyond noticing animals.

"I knew it was true," he said thickly, his back to Melissa as she approached.

"Jed—knew what was true?"

109

"That—that she'd bewitched him. That he's just forgetting my mother altogether and running after her, like, like . . ."

"Jed, come on! It's *nice* for your father, I think, being interested in someone again."

He turned on her furiously. "Oh, is it? And nice to be left, too, I suppose, like she's obviously leaving him. You know what that'll do to him, don't you? Back to the bottle. She must know that! She's evil, Melissa, evil and cruel . . ."

Neither of them had seen Seth come around the corner of the cottage and stand there, watching and listening. He strode between them and faced his son. "Who's evil and cruel?" he bellowed.

"That woman," Jed bellowed back defiantly. "That Rhiannon—witch woman."

Seth Ellison pulled back his arm as if to strike his son. But Melissa, who'd been there once before when he had hit Jed, seized it, shouting, "No!"

Seth dropped his arm. "Listen," he said to Jed, his voice low and intense. "I don't want to hear you say anything against her. It's true that she doesn't talk much about herself; I don't know any more about where she's from than anyone else. But she's a good woman, no matter what people say. Kind and sweet and—and generous."

"That was Mom," said Jed bitterly, almost sobbing. "No one else. What would Mom think?"

"Jed, your mother's dead," Melissa said, stepping toward him. "She's been dead for years, she's . . ."

But he cut her off, shouting. "I suppose," he said, "you'd be delighted if *your* father took up with someone. Your mother's only been dead a few months, but I suppose you're all ready for someone to move into her place. And I thought you loved her like I loved my mother. I suppose you'd dance at their wedding!"

110

Tears sprang to Melissa's eyes, and she turned, running. But she wasn't fast enough to miss Jed's saying cruelly to his father, "You better go read the note the witch woman left you. Then see what you think of her."

Melissa ran to the brook, where both dogs, dripping water, scrambled to their feet to greet her. She fell to her knees and threw her arms around Ulfin, sobbing into his wet fur. He let her lean on him, and Linnet reached across his back to lick the tears off Melissa's face as fast as they fell. She nudged Melissa's chin with her nose, wagging her tail in circles and dancing, as if ready to play. Ulfin held his paw out to Melissa and then stretched his head toward hers, giving her face one of his long, slow, infinitely gentle licks. His eyes looked sadly into her eyes, but the flecks in them—green, yellow, red—seemed to burn. Linnet nudged Melissa again, and then they both ran ahead, as if asking her to follow—so she did, her face dry of tears now.

They led her beyond the brook, into the woods on another side of Round Top, and then down through more woods, heavily leafy and hot—oaks, maples, beeches, a few clumps of birch here and there where it was more open. And then over a stone wall, into a darker forest—hemlocks mostly, and other evergreens. Melissa was at first so numb with grief and confusion that she didn't think of where she was going, and then gradually, as she came to herself more, she followed because she didn't know where she was and knew she would be lost without the dogs.

But Ulfin never got me lost before, she thought, remembering all the times he had led her and Jed into the woods behind Gran's to the hermit's tumbledown house.

Suddenly both dogs stopped and sat one on each side of her, panting in the heavy, evergreen-scented air.

Melissa frowned. On all sides were pines, with little spiky

111

mayflowers making a green-and-white pattern in the brown-needled forest floor. Her feet sank deep into the fragrant needles, their scent mingling with the sweet mayflowers'; the combination was as strong as jasmine in the still heat. The pines were of all sizes, but perfectly shaped; ahead of her was a heap of rocks . . .

Frowning more deeply, she went closer to it. It was hard to tell now, with no snow on the ground—but—yes—she climbed up on a rock and peered through a small chink—peered down into a cave, neat and certainly touched by humans, for there were wooden shelves, stone candle sconces, an odd stone shelf . . .

She realized she was remembering rather than seeing, for the light in the cave was very dim. But she knew where she was now: at the hermit's root cellar—his temple, the Temple of the Old Ways.

And then a shape inside the root cellar stirred and Melissa saw a white-robed figure standing sideways, apparently not noticing her, holding a small harp, strumming it, singing . . .

. . . Melissa blinked. The dogs were gone—was Rhiannon? For of course it was Rhiannon in the temple. The pine scent seemed stronger; mingled with the mayflower, it was again overwhelming. It had also grown very much hotter, although there was a breeze cutting through the heat, arguing with it. There was music, Melissa was sure, and then out of the forest came two lines of people, one from the direction of Round Top, from which she herself had come, the other from back toward Gran's and the village. The Round Top group were dressed in robes and laden with crude farming tools, musical instruments, bolts of thickly woven cloth, clay pots, gold jewelry. One carried a lamb, another a kid—Dian? But it couldn't be. The people looked foreign, somehow, and tired, as if they had come from very far away. And then she noticed that the first four formed a rough circle as they walked, and that each of them with great reverence was carrying one of her grandmother's silver plates.

She moved toward them, but then the other line of people closed in and she had to stay back, and she saw who they were—Melissa rubbed her eyes. Why, there was everyone she knew: Gran, and Tommy, and Joan Savage and her parents, and Mr.-Ellison-the-Selectman, and Miss Laurent, and the Tituses, and Mrs.-Ellison-in-the-school-office, and Mrs.-Ellison-the-librarian, and Jed, and Seth. She ran toward Jed, wanting to apologize, to be friends again, but he seemed not to see her; he went right past, as did the others, as if she were invisible.

The two groups stopped at the temple and faced each other solemnly. Then after a moment they moved on, each group going in the direction from which the other had come, except —except—

Except for Jed, who stood, head bowed, outside the temple, and who then turned un-Jed-like toward her, holding out his hand . . .

. . . And then Linnet was licking her hands, quickly, as if to wake her, and Rhiannon was bathing her face with cool water and saying, "You must have fainted with the heat, child. Wait, do not move just yet. There—better?"

Melissa looked around dazedly. "I thought—I thought . . ." she began. Then she changed her mind and said, "Has anyone else been here? Besides us, I mean? You and me and the dogs?"

"No," said Rhiannon soothingly, "no one." Then she smiled. "The music has been here," she said, and Melissa noticed again that Rhiannon was wearing white—though not a robe

113

—and had her harp with her. "Melissa," said Rhiannon, holding out her hand and helping Melissa up, "you know this place, do you not?"

Melissa nodded, although she was sure it was unnecessary, that Rhiannon knew.

"Old and New meeting," said Rhiannon softly, touching Melissa's hair. "The second lesson. The music is the beginning of the door between for you. It could be for Jed, too, although he is not as you are; he cannot see what you have seen . . ."

"I don't understand," said Melissa, and then prosaically, remembering, "The note—Jed's father . . ."

"I know," said Rhiannon. "But he is close to healed now, child; he will recover. And I will see him before I leave, many times. Melissa, listen: you are one of us; the dogs know. You can open the door between. There will come a great test . . ."

Melissa felt as if she were still mostly in the dream—or whatever it was—that she'd been in a few minutes earlier. Rhiannon's words didn't always make sense; Melissa found herself feeling what she meant more than actually understanding it. Jed couldn't see, Rhiannon had said, what she had seen. That must be the deep valley, Melissa thought, and instantly, when she thought it, it was as if she were there again, watching the row of tired-looking people enter it and then come toward her. She heard Rhiannon's song fleetingly and knew without being surprised or alarmed that she was watching the people, with their tools and the silver plates, move from the valley across time and space until they were in Fours Crossing.

And then they faded—vanished—and the second group of people, the people she knew, were there in their place. But something was wrong; they seemed shallow, rootless; their tools were sharp and hard and cruel and the plates—the plates hung behind them as on Gran's wall, but out of order, tarnished, and forgotten.

"What—what test?" she managed to ask, opening her eyes dazedly—had they been closed, then?

But Rhiannon and Linnet were gone and there was the sound of someone crashing through the woods; a rather breathless Jed appeared, scattering pine needles as he burst through the underbrush with Ulfin—still no Linnet, though, no Rhiannon. "There you are," he said to Melissa. "Ulfin showed me. Why on earth did you come here? Look, I'm sorry . . ."

The rest of the vision faded.

12

"I really am," Jed was saying while Melissa rubbed her eyes and tried to force herself back into her surroundings. "I'm sorry that I yelled at you, anyway." He kicked at a stone. "But I'm not sorry for saying what I said about Rhiannon. I still think what I thought, Melissa, and nothing's going to change that. I—oh, come on, let's go back, at least." He glanced at the root cellar. "This place gives me the creeps, doesn't it you?"

Still too dazed to answer, Melissa followed Jed along the path he'd come on, toward Fours Crossing this time instead of Round Top. The path looked very different from the last time she'd seen it, snow-covered and icy, the day they'd been rescued from the root cellar.

"You what?" asked Melissa, trying now to concentrate on Jed. "You started to say something."

"Nothing." Then he turned to her. "Well, that's not true. It's just that—that it's almost as if she's bewitched you, too. Or as if you've sort of adopted her as your mother. That's what Joan Savage said, anyway."

"Joan Savage!" Melissa exploded, more vehemently than

she would have expected herself to. "What's she got to do with it?"

Jed suddenly turned away. "Nothing," he said. "I was just talking to her, that's all."

Melissa walked faster, pushing past Jed and walking ahead of him, her thoughts and feelings a tangle. Maybe it was true, at least a little; there were certainly things about Rhiannon that reminded her of her mother. But so what if they did? Certainly that had nothing to do with being bewitched—whatever that really meant in Jed's vocabulary.

As for Joan Savage . . .

Jed caught up with her. "Jealous?" he asked, grinning. "H'm?"

"Why should I be?" she snapped. "You have to care a lot about someone to be jealous."

"Oh, so you don't care!" he snapped back. "Fine." He whistled to Ulfin, who had been nosing around at the side of the path. "Come on, Ulf, let's go home."

But Ulfin jumped on him and then ran to Melissa, jumping on her, too.

"He wants us to make up," Melissa said softly, rubbing Ulfin's ears. "Don't you, Ulf?"

As if in answer, Ulfin jumped back to Jed again, licking his face—a Linnet-lick, really, short and fast.

Jed laughed. "Oh, all right," he said. "All *right*, Ulfin." He held out his hand to Melissa. "Sorry again," he said. "It must be all the heat. Friends?"

"Friends," she answered, and shook his hand. "And"—she turned away—"it wasn't true about not caring."

"It wasn't true about Joan Savage, either," he said cheerfully. "I mean, it's true I talked to her, and it's true she said that about Rhiannon and your mother, but it's not true that I—you know."

Melissa nodded. "The last time we had a fight," she said, "it was because you'd begun to figure out about the plate and spring and everything, and you . . ."

"I had an awful feeling something terrible was going on," he said, completing her sentence. "Right. But what does that have to do with . . ."

"Don't you see?" she said, suddenly desperate. "Now I'm the one who feels that something terrible is going on—oh, not Rhiannon; I'm surer than ever that she's good. I think she's trying to warn us—me, anyway. But I can't get you to listen!"

They had reached the stone wall that separated the field behind Gran's house from the woods. Jed leaned against it, facing her, his face serious again. "I think something's going on, too," he said. "But I don't agree with you that Rhiannon's trying to warn us. I think she's the cause. So I guess we're just going to have to . . . What's that?"

Someone was running across the field, shouting to them—Tommy.

"Jed! Melissa!" they heard when he was close enough. "It's the jury. They're coming back. Mr. Savage says he'll drive us to Hiltonville!"

It was a quiet group in Mr. Savage's car—Jed, Melissa, Tommy, Gran—plus Mr. Savage, driving. Seth was nowhere to be found, nor was Rhiannon, and they didn't dare take the time to hunt for them. Melissa, squeezed in the back seat between Jed and Tommy, could feel her own heart pounding wildly and wondered if theirs were, too. "Well, we'll know soon, anyway," Gran had said when they piled into the car, but Melissa could see from the look on her face that Gran was as worried as she was. What would happen if Mr. Savage was wrong and the hermit went free? Would he go back to being Forest Keeper? Would the town Selectmen let him? Melissa wasn't even sure if they had anything to say about it, since the position was hereditary. But if the hermit wasn't Forest Keeper, who would be? The only other Dunns, as far as she knew, were she and her father, and they, Gran had explained, were just several-times-removed relatives.

Why, she wondered nervously, am I thinking about all this?

In her mind, she could see the hermit in front of her as he'd stood once in the root cellar, robes flowing. *I will shake you till your bones rattle!* he'd threatened. *If you do not curb that tongue, I will curb it for you . . .*

They couldn't let him go, they just couldn't.

I have taken spring, he had told them, *and I will keep it until the traitor villagers are gone from this sacred place, and the place and you are purified. Only then will I allow spring to come—only when the Old Ways will no more be mocked . . . You will help me . . .*

Rhiannon's voice came back to her then, and the lines of people coming out of darkness: *You are one of us . . . You can open the door between. There will come a great test . . .*

"Well, here we are," said Mr. Savage, pulling the car up to the courthouse.

"Good luck," Tommy whispered as they got out of the car. He squeezed Melissa's hand and looked anxiously into Jed's face. Jed's mouth was set and grim, but his words were confident. "It'll be all right," he said, looking at Melissa. "It'll be fine. They couldn't be so dumb as to let him go."

But Melissa's whole body felt cold and numb as they walked up the steps. As they crossed the lobby, her eyes were drawn involuntarily to the door leading to the basement stairs where the jail was. Was he down there, waiting also? For a second—only a second, as had happened once or twice in the root cellar—she had a pang of sympathy for him. *Poor lonely old man*, she knew Gran would say, even though Gran would also be the first person to want him locked up forever.

"Come on," Jed whispered, pulling at her arm, and they followed the others into the courtroom.

Mr. O'Callahan was pacing back and forth at the front of the room, anxiously for him. There were fewer spectators than before, although the room was almost full, and this time no one spoke. The court officers were standing around as usual, but today they looked more expectant than bored. Mr. Savage whispered to one of them, then came back to Gran and said, "We're in plenty of time."

Melissa followed the others to a bench, staying as close to Gran as she could. "I wish Daddy were still here," she whispered when Gran patted her shoulder, and at that, Gran put an arm around her, whispering, "You know he wishes he could have stayed," and held her close. But even that couldn't warm her, or make her feel really there. It was like being in a play, or watching one; nothing was quite real; her body was there but the rest of her wasn't. Someone tapped her shoulder and she turned around to look into Rhiannon's eyes. "Steady," Rhiannon whispered. "Steady. There is great strength in you, Melissa; hold fast to it." Then she sat down near them but not on the same bench—not far from the dock, Melissa noticed.

"Dad's not here," Jed whispered.

"Maybe he wouldn't want to see Rhiannon," Melissa somehow managed to whisper back, aching for her own father, "after the note."

"I guess," Jed answered. "Who needs him, anyway?"

You do, Melissa's mind said, but she kept silent.

"All rise!" the clerk called, and Melissa got stiffly, mechanically to her feet with the others as Judge Cabot came into the room. Then the small door at the side opened and the hermit was led in, wearing his everyday black robe for the first time in court, instead of regular clothes. His eyes darted rapidly around the courtroom, settled for a moment on Rhiannon, and then found Melissa and Jed; his lips twisted in a mirthless smile.

There was a rustle behind them, and Seth, sober but a bit more rumpled than he'd been wont to be recently, awkwardly climbed over outstretched feet and pushed his way onto the bench beside Jed. "You're here, lad," he panted. "I looked all over for you." He patted Jed's knee. "Easy, son," he said. "They won't let him go."

"Of course not," Jed said lightly. "They aren't fools."

"Right," said Seth. "That's m'boy." His head turned, searching the room.

"Over there," said Jed, indicating Rhiannon with an outwardly indifferent toss of his chin.

Seth gave Jed a look and then nodded.

Well, thought Melissa, momentarily distracted, maybe that's an apology. At least they're speaking to each other. Then she felt Gran's arm tighten around her, and the jury came in, stone-faced, eyes front, looking at no one, least of all the hermit—who was leaning forward, his eyes scanning their features. Mr. O'Callahan's face darkened, Mr. Davis looked hopeful, Mr. Savage frowned, and Melissa found it suddenly impossible to breathe. She could feel her pulse beating hard in her throat, her ears. I wonder if I'm going to faint, she thought wildly, then scolded herself, thinking of her mother: "Be sensible, Melissa"—and knew she wouldn't faint after all. Mum's here, she thought then; somehow, she's with me . . .

"Mr. Foreman," said the sparrow-faced clerk, "have you reached a verdict on the larceny charge?"

A tall, dark-suited man—"He looks like an undertaker," Tommy whispered—got up. "We have," he intoned.

"Sounds like one, too," Jed whispered back, but Melissa found herself unable to join in their suppressed nervous giggles.

"The defendant will rise," ordered the clerk.

Mr. O'Callahan moved closer to the dock and lankily motioned the hermit to stand up. The old man stood very straight, his black robe flowing loosely around him. There was an odd kind of dignity on his deeply lined face as he stood there tensely waiting.

The clerk tipped his head toward the jury foreman, looking more sparrow-like than ever. "And what is your verdict?" he asked.

"It's as bad as the Oscars," said Seth in a nervous whisper.

"The envelope, *please!*" giggled Tommy. "Only there isn't one . . ."

"Shut up, can't you?" Jed whispered fiercely, and Tommy shrank.

By that time the foreman had already started speaking: "We find the defendant, Eli John Dunn, guilty as charged . . ."

Someone gasped; someone else—Gran? Jed?—gripped Melissa's hand.

". . . of the larceny of the plate."

A low wail, so quiet at first it was almost not there, like a strong wind starting slowly, came from the dock . . .

"Order!" Judge Cabot snapped, pounding with her gavel.

"So say you, so say you all?" asked the clerk, and the jurors, nodding, answered "Yes" in unison.

"And," chirped the clerk, nodding back at them as if he approved, "have you reached a verdict on the kidnapping charge?"

"We have," said the foreman, a little more firmly this time.

"On the kidnapping charge we find the defendant—we find the defendant not guilty by reason of insanity."

For a moment the silence in the room was like the stillness in the air before a thunderstorm. Then there was a buzz of voices—and under it, the windlike wail rose.

Melissa closed her eyes. *Watch him,* she prayed; *please, please watch him . . .*

"So say you, so say you all?" asked the clerk; he had to speak more loudly now.

"We do," said the jurors.

"Your honor," said Mr. Davis, raising his voice also, "I—"

But the hermit interrupted him with a shriek and, thrashing wildly, nearly broke away from his guards. Gran put her arm around Melissa; Seth drew closer to Jed. Above the general din, Judge Cabot said, "Restrain the prisoner!" and the guards seized the hermit again, forcing him to sit down. Then Judge Cabot rose and quieted the court, and when most people were seated again—Gran's arm still firmly around Melissa—the judge said, "Because of the complexity of the verdict and the necessity of imposing a dual sentence, this court is adjourned until tomorrow morning at nine-thirty a.m., at which time I will hear arguments on disposition."

"That means," Mr. Savage began, "that it's going to be hard for her to decide what to do with him because he's got a not-guilty-by-reason-of-insanity on one charge and a guilty on the other . . ."

But no one listened to him, and his voice trailed off as the hermit, shaking his gnarled fist and his eyes spitting pain and fire, was led from the courtroom.

Gran, Melissa, Jed, and Seth sat in stunned, uncertain silence.

And Rhiannon gathered her cloak around her and ran swiftly out, well ahead of everyone else.

13

Dinner was a thrown-together affair of cold leftover ham, salad, and bread. "I'd planned a cold soup," said Gran apologetically, "but there just wasn't time."

"This is fine, Miz Dunn," Seth said; he and Jed had come for dinner—awkwardly, as if they'd reached a truce, but a tentative one. Seth reached for another piece of bread and piled ham on it. "Sticks to the ribs better'n soup any day."

"More, Melissa?" asked Gran, passing her the platter.

Melissa shook her head. She'd barely been able to eat one thin sandwich as it was. "May I be excused?" she asked.

Gran looked dubiously at Melissa's unfinished salad. "Well," she said, "there *is* dessert, too, you know."

"I think we're just too wrought up to eat, Miz Dunn," said Jed, pushing back his chair. "It's very good, but—well, maybe we could have dessert later."

Gran sighed. "Well, run along, then, you two." She got up, patting Pride and Joy on her way to the stove. "Coffee, Seth?"

"Please," said Seth, pushing back his chair. "And *I* wouldn't mind dessert now, even if the young 'uns don't want it."

"Then you shall have it," said Gran, putting the coffee on, as Jed and Melissa slipped out the back door, and opening the refrigerator to take out the lemon sponge pudding Melissa knew was cooling there.

There was a bright moon, on its way to being full, with clouds scudding across its face. Melissa and Jed walked silently across Gran's newly mowed field to the stone wall at the edge of the woods. Ulfin, who'd been waiting for Jed on the back steps, padded silently along between them, reaching up every now and then to nuzzle first Melissa's hand, then Jed's.

"I wish," said Jed, as they sat on the warm ground, their backs to the wall, Ulfin watchful in front of them, "that we could have read more of those pages from the history book."

Melissa nodded. The night seemed to press down on her, heavily; maybe the clouds mean it's going to rain at last, she thought, knowing that she was wrong. But there was some comfort in a logical explanation, even if she sensed it wasn't true.

"I'll be happier after tomorrow," Jed said, idly patting Ulfin, who grunted appreciatively.

"Me too," said Melissa.

"Did you see the way Rhiannon ran out after him?"

"Ran out, anyway," Melissa said carefully. "You can't really say she ran out *after* him. Your father," she said, "seems better now."

"I guess," Jed answered. "A little, anyway."

"I wonder," said Melissa shyly, "if we'll ever be like that. Having fights with someone, being told it's all over."

"I won't be," Jed said. "Either you love someone or you don't, it seems to me. None of this back and forth."

"I'm not sure it's as easy as all that," Melissa said, watching a silver-edged cloud move across the moon. "Like—well, like with Rhiannon. If she does have to go away—well, maybe she wants to stay with your dad, but she can't."

"Seems dumb to me," Jed said stubbornly. "Like I said, either you love someone or you don't. If you do, you stay with them, even if you can't."

Melissa laughed. "Oh, Jed," she said, "that doesn't make any sense."

"Well," he said, standing up, "it makes sense to *me*. Can't's not much of a word anyway."

"Gran would say that," Melissa said. "Sometimes you're a lot like her."

"She half brought me up," he said gruffly, his face in darkness. "More than half. You're lucky to have her for a gran."

"You've known her longer than I have," said Melissa. "Known her better, anyway."

"You knew your own mother," he said abruptly, "better and longer than I knew mine. So we're even." He sat down again, looking at the moon. "Ever want to go up there?" he asked.

Melissa shook her head; then, realizing he probably hadn't seen her, she said, "No."

"I have." He stretched his arms wide. "I used to dream about flying there—oh, not in a spaceship or anything scientific like that—flying there like a bird, a hawk, maybe . . ."

"Like that little sparrow hawk Rhiannon saved from the flood?" said Melissa. "He looks like such a smart bird."

"Hawks are smart," said Jed. "And strong. And—and good, somehow, even if they are birds of prey. At least that one seems to be." His arms dropped and he turned to her. "Melissa, he's so *evil*, the hermit. Don't you feel it? I mean, more than before. As if—as if he's more poisoned than ever by what's wrong with him . . ."

"Or as if," she said, almost whispering, "nothing's wrong

with him at all, not insanity, anyway, but—well, maybe like with the first Eli, something . . ."

". . . something no one understands," Jed interrupted, "or can understand now. Something out of another world or another time."

Melissa wondered if she should tell Jed about the valley she'd dreamed. And the rows of people she'd seen coming from it later, when she'd fainted in the woods.

But Jed pointed up to the sky, interrupting her thoughts. "Look," he said.

An especially large cloud sailed across the moon, blotting it out, making Gran's field in front of them and the woods behind them darker than the valley Melissa had been about to describe. They could see nothing, not even outlines or masses—as if no one's left in the world but us, Melissa thought.

There was a sharp movement in front of them, and a low growl.

Melissa put out her hand and felt Ulfin's neck hair rising stiffly; Jed's hand reached for Ulfin at the same time.

"What is it, Ulfin?" Jed whispered. "What is it?"

Prickles chased each other up and down Melissa's spine.

"Ulfin?" said Jed—for the dog moved suddenly forward.

And then he threw back his head and howled, more wolf than dog—a long, rising howl that reached a peak and broke as it descended, eerily.

Then Gran's voice came across the field, normal, calling them in.

That night Melissa lay restlessly tossing, driving Pride and Joy to the rug from his usual place at the foot of her bed. For a while she tried reading, but her mind wouldn't concentrate.

She tried doing a crossword puzzle; she solved several cryptograms in a book her father had sent her; she even tried drawing pictures—but nothing took her mind off the next day at all.

What's Judge Cabot doing, she wondered suddenly. Does she have any idea yet what to do with him? Or is she wide awake, too, staring at the moon, thinking about tomorrow?

Melissa got out of bed—it seemed a little cooler—and went to her window.

The moon was free of clouds now, shining softly, bathing Gran's delicate columbines with its soft light.

And showing her Ulfin, lying protectively under her window again; he looked up and wagged his tail once as she leaned out.

But why, she thought this time, climbing restlessly back to bed. Why is he guarding me again?

"This should be the last bit of school you'll miss," Mr. Savage said to Melissa and Jed cheerfully the next morning as they, with Gran, climbed the steps to the courthouse once more; Seth and Rhiannon, apparently somewhat reconciled, had gone ahead in Seth's truck. "There's no need, you know, to worry," he went on. "There's no chance now that he'll be freed. It's just a matter of where and for how long he'll be put away."

There was a flurry of activity ahead of them, near the doors. Two men with plastic press cards clipped to their lapels burst out of the lobby and pounded down the steps, racing for the cluster of pay phones on the sidewalk.

Melissa looked at Jed. He had gone suddenly pale.

"Wonder what all that's about?" said Mr. Savage, frowning slightly. "Well, probably nothing to do with us. There are other trials going on here, you know—we're not the only pebbles on the beach, or maybe I should say trees in the forest, since we're miles from any beach up here. Shall we go in?"

Melissa managed a feeble smile and followed Mr. Savage into the lobby. Left foot, right foot; left foot, right foot, she forced herself to think; left foot, right foot. Her legs were so leaden it was almost necessary for her to say the words out loud to force herself to move.

The lobby was as active as a disturbed anthill. Knots of people, excitedly whispering, clustered by the elevators and near the doors. Every other person, it seemed, was a policeman, with more arriving at the side doors and coming up from the stairs leading to the basement jail. As soon as Melissa and Jed came in, Chief Dupres broke away from a uniformed group talking to the lobby guard and came up to them.

Melissa's mouth went dry as Chief Dupres laid one hand on her shoulder and another on Jed's, looking at Gran gravely over their heads.

"It's a hard thing to have to tell you," he said heavily. "But —well, it seems the hermit's escaped."

14

Fear settled over the valley, thick as the growing heat.

Rhiannon, it turned out, had been the last person to see the hermit; she'd spent a couple of hours with him after the trial, while he ate his dinner. After letting her out, the guard on duty had spent the night at his desk outside the small block of cells, nursing a bad cold; he hadn't, he admitted shamefacedly, gone back to the hermit's cell after Rhiannon had left, nor had he checked it during the night as he was supposed to do.

And in the morning, when he'd taken the hermit's breakfast in, the old man was gone, one hinge of his cell door hanging loose and broken, and two of the bars meant to protect the cell's small window bent apart.

"Not enough room for more'n a skinny kid to get out," Chief Dupres's sergeant, Charley, reported to Mr. Titus in the general store that afternoon, when everyone was back in the village, doors bolted and windows shut.

"It's that woman," Mr. Titus said darkly, his face weasel-sharp, "with her witchy ways."

"Oh, come on, Alex," said Frank Grange of the Highway

Department, sipping root beer in the corner. "What do you think she did—magicked him out?"

"I wouldn't be surprised," Mr. Titus muttered, while Charley laughed.

"Next thing you know," Frank said good-naturedly, putting down the empty bottle, "you'll be seeing ladies on broomsticks. Good thing it's a while till Halloween. Take care, Eleanor," he said to Mrs. Titus as he held the door open for an incoming customer. "Better watch that man of yours or he'll be off to join a coven next." He shook his head as he left. "Witchy ways, indeed. Some folks'll believe anything."

But Mr. Titus wasn't, as it turned out, the only suspicious person in Fours Crossing. Mrs.-Ellison-in-the-school-office, duplicating exams on the library's copier, said to Mrs.-Ellison-the-librarian, "Well, I don't see how it's possible, either, but they say she was the last one who saw him, so it must be her, mustn't it? Course I don't hold with what some folks are saying about some kind of special powers, but . . ."

"But it *has* been unseasonably hot since she arrived, and that's a fact," said Mrs.-Ellison-the-librarian. "Still, of course, there's no such thing . . ."

It was some time around then that the match was dropped into the dry grass and the whispers sped through the village as fast and as destructively as fire, soon so out of control that Chief Dupres reluctantly agreed to send Charley up to Round Top to seek Rhiannon out and question her.

But Rhiannon wasn't there.

Nor was there any sign of her—or of anyone else—at the root cellar or the Keeper's House.

"Makes it worse, like," Chief Dupres said, questioning Jed and Melissa after the first day of exams. "If you kids know where she is . . ."

They shook their heads.

"It'd be better for Miss Jones if she came to see me," said Chief Dupres gently. "Those rumors are getting mighty ugly —I don't like the feel of things at all."

A day later, much to Melissa's relief, Rhiannon at last appeared in the chief's office and spent the morning closeted with him and Charley. "Says she'll stick around," the chief was quoted by the local newspaper as telling a reporter, "and right now I've got nothing to charge her with. Sure, she's a suspect in aiding him to escape, but long as she reports to me every day like she's promised, there's nothing more to be done unless someone files a real complaint against her. I'm not going to—there's no hard evidence. All we've got is a warrant for the old man, and that's what we're working on."

The rumors died down a little after that, but Rhiannon was still unwelcome in the village, and whispers and stares followed her wherever she went. Except for reporting to the chief every day, she stayed on Round Top.

"There is great danger now," she told Jed and Melissa when they went to see her—Jed reluctantly—the day after she'd first gone to the chief. "He is threatening the village; I can feel it. He will try again to force a return to the past, to the Old Ways, unchanged by the New. I do not know how he will do it, nor do I know all his powers. But he is obsessed with it. Each time I saw him in Hiltonville, each time I spoke to him, he would talk of nothing else but restoring the Old Ways."

"Did he ever say anything to you about escaping?" Jed asked, eyeing her narrowly.

Rhiannon shook her head. "He had no need. I knew what he was plotting. And no"—she smiled sadly at Jed—"I had nothing to do with it, though you will not believe that, I know."

Jed looked embarrassed. "It'd help," he said, "if we knew why you went to see him so much."

"To change his mind," she said swiftly, "as I have told Melissa. To show him that he must give in, that he must grow and change. But I could not reach him." Rhiannon stroked Linnet, who was lying beside her, next to Ulfin. Linnet had been washing Ulfin's face and he'd been lying still for her, as if reveling in the quick, thorough strokes of her tongue. "They are good friends, these two," said Rhiannon, smiling at the dogs. "Sometimes I fear for them—for us all. There is no telling what he will try. You must keep him always with you," she said to Jed and Melissa, touching Ulfin.

"He's been sleeping under my window," said Melissa.

Rhiannon nodded. "Good. You will need guarding more than Jed. Not"—she smiled—"because you are a girl, but because you are a Dunn and live where you live." She touched Melissa's shoulder. "Do not be afraid. Only watchful. Ulfin will keep you from harm. And my little one here"— she nodded toward Linnet—"will lead you when the time comes."

"Can't we find him?" Jed asked desperately before Melissa could ask Rhiannon what she meant. "I mean, we can't go on forever dreading him and just—just sort of waiting for him to do something."

"He will act soon enough," said Rhiannon. "Perhaps at Midsummer; he may feel his power strongest then."

"Midsummer," said Jed. "But Midsummer Day's when they postponed graduation to."

Rhiannon looked momentarily startled, but all she said was, "It is also an ancient time of power." Then she told them, "Stay together, as much as you can. You will be stronger together and with the dogs. We must watch Dian, too," she added as the little goat turned from where she'd been browsing near the brook and forced her way between Ulfin and Linnet, butting Linnet playfully.

"I don't understand," said Jed. "What do the animals have to do with it?"

But Rhiannon, instead of answering, offered scones.

That night, after the air had hung still and hot all afternoon, there was a tremendous thunderstorm, with high wind and hailstones as big as golf balls, but no real rain. The hail made craters in more than one farmer's field, pasting the few tentatively sprouting seedlings back into the ground. The wind stripped the leaves from oaks and lettuces alike, and whipped daisies into dry whirlpools. A mare got loose in the storm, was struck by lightning and killed—and the next morning children sang "Witchy, witchy, witchy" outside the school while Melissa struggled to write the essay part of her English exam.

Miss Laurent, proctoring, closed the window, but the sound still came through.

"It says here," said Joan Savage after school, pulling a thin book out of her school bag, "that people used to think witches caused bad weather, deformed births, and blasted crops, whatever they are. How silly!"

"Blasted means destroyed," said Jed, who had joined them. "Withered. Let's see that."

Melissa, angry, left them and spent an hour cleaning Gran's henhouse, unasked. Then she found a misshapen egg under one of the roosts and ran inside trembling, telling herself it would be ridiculous to scream.

"If she was in jail," Mr. Titus was saying darkly when Melissa went to the store for Gran late the next afternoon, "then we'd know, wouldn't we, if she was causing it all?"

"I dunno, Alex," said Frank Grange. "Seems to me if you believe in that stuff, you've got to believe she could do anything she wanted, even from jail. Look at the Salem witches"

—here he winked at Mrs. Titus—"why, they were said to be able to be in two places at once, like—sleeping quiet in their beds like good wives and running around the woods with the Devil at the same time. Dunno as it'd do any good to put her in jail."

"I'm saying to put her in jail only if she won't leave and take him with her."

"Oh, good Lord, Alex." Frank shook his head, his face more serious now. "Amounts to the same thing, doesn't it?"

"Then you won't sign?" asked Mr. Titus, with a glance toward Melissa.

"No, I won't," said Frank. "If this town's to have a witch-hunt, you can darn well count me out." And he stalked out of the store, slamming the door behind him.

"Sign what?" asked Melissa, putting the sugar and yeast Gran had asked for onto the counter.

"Oh, nothing that concerns you, little lady," said Mr. Titus. "Just a grownup thing, that's all. That'll be three dollars and sixty-five cents."

Melissa looked hopefully at Mrs. Titus.

"Well, Alex, I don't see why she can't know," Mrs. Titus said, her small wrinkled face looking worried and embarrassed at the same time. "It's a petition, dear, asking the police to order Miss Jones to leave town, and to arrest her if she refuses. Mr. Titus and some other folks are worried that she might be—well, doing harm—hiding the hermit, and that. If she leaves, they figure he will, too. And if she's in jail, she won't be able to help him, or"—she glanced at her husband—"harm us."

Melissa summoned up all her courage and tried to stare both of the Tituses down. "Do you mean to say people in Fours Crossing still believe in *witches*?" she asked scornfully.

Mrs. Titus looked away.

"Not maybe actual witches so much," said Mr. Titus placidly, putting the sugar and yeast in a paper bag. "Just believe in being careful, is all."

"The dumb thing," Melissa said to Gran later, exasperated, "is that I know perfectly well they don't really believe in witches. What they're doing is using the *idea* of witches as an excuse, Mr. Titus especially, to make people more suspicious, just because so many people don't like her in the first place."

"They're scared, Melissa," said Gran, but she seemed troubled, too. "And they want to blame someone."

"And my poor father's out there trying to raise money for this dumb town—oh, Gran, I didn't mean that! At least I . . ."

"It's all right, lambie," Gran said, patting her hand. She smoothed Melissa's hair. "It's a sad thing, but—well, even nice folks aren't always what they seem to be. Like chickens, some people are, pecking at anyone who's a bit different from themselves. You and I, we know Rhiannon better than most folks here. The people who talk the loudest know her least, I daresay."

But somehow even Gran's wisdom couldn't comfort Melissa. And she was surer than ever that underneath the cloak of the town's suspicion of Rhiannon, the hermit was waiting until he knew the time was right for him to strike.

15

Exams ended on a day of blinding heat, with no rain at the end of it, even though again rain seemed to threaten. The next day was hazy and close. It wasn't a real school day but instead a time for cleaning out desks and rehearsing graduation music. For the Sevens and Eights, too, there was a special assembly, during which the Eights read a mock will, leaving gifts to the Sevens. To peals of laughter, Jed left Tommy a box of mothballs for his acorn cap, which Tommy still wore on all but the hottest days. He left Melissa his desk, at which Melissa felt mingled pleasure and guilt, sure that Tommy must have wanted it—and then she wondered if she'd still be in Fours Crossing next year to use it or if she'd be back in Boston with her father.

After assembly, they were free until graduation, still nearly a week away, while exams were graded and the school was cleaned and decorated. There was nothing official to do till the party the night before graduation—a Fours Crossing tradition, Tommy and Jed explained to Melissa, with a bonfire and a picnic partway up Round Top and a midnight parade around the village.

"Sounds like fun," Melissa said; they were all three standing on the school porch after assembly, reluctant to move in the heat. "Where's the custom come from?"

"Who knows?" Tommy said listlessly, his cap protruding from his back pocket and his box of mothballs on the floor beside him. "No one even really knows what happens at the picnic part till they go to it when they're in seventh grade. And no one who's been ever tells. Of course," he said mischievously, perking up a little and glancing at Jed, "if someone who went last year *wanted* to tell . . ."

"Not on your life," said Jed, cuffing him lightly. "What a question."

"Just trying," Tommy said, shrugging. He stood up and stretched. "I s'pose I'd better get going," he said. "My mother wants to take me to Hiltonville to buy a suit for graduation. You'd think she could wait till *next* year, when it's really my turn. Or at least wait for a cooler day—hey, look!"

Melissa followed Tommy's pointing finger and saw Ulfin trotting purposefully across the green, straight toward the school.

"He's sure got something on his mind," Tommy said. "Well, see you." He picked up the mothballs and ran down the steps, patting Ulfin as he passed—or trying to; Ulfin ignored him and went straight to Jed, nudging him urgently with his nose.

"What is it, boy?" Jed asked, kneeling and taking Ulfin's head between his hands. "What?"

Ulfin made a low noise in his throat, more rumble than growl. But there was no mistaking his meaning as he tossed his head and turned to Melissa, nudging her, too, and then running down the steps again, looking back at them over his shoulder and barking urgently.

"All right, Ulf," Jed said, after glancing at Melissa, who resignedly shouldered her school bag, full of odds and ends of leftovers from the three months she'd spent in Fours Crossing School. "We're coming."

Ulfin began to run as soon as Jed and Melissa were down on the street—around the green and across the bridge . . .

"Round Top?" said Jed as Ulfin paused, waiting impatiently for them to catch up.

Melissa shook her head, for instead of turning, Ulfin ran straight ahead, up the road to Gran's.

And past Gran's, where Melissa left her school bag by the back steps, and across the field to the stone wall, and over the stone wall into the woods.

Except for its being so hot, Melissa thought, longing for a drink of water as she struggled to keep up, it could be last March—for Ulfin seemed to be leading them through the woods to the Keeper's House. But of course the forest had looked very different then, when the heavy snow had made tents of the lower branches of hemlock trees and the bare deciduous trees had stood out in silhouette against the gray sky. Now the deciduous trees were thickly green and the path, largely unused, was so overgrown Melissa doubted that even Jed would be able to find his way without Ulfin.

Ulfin stopped suddenly, in front of the second stone wall, at the edge of the forest that was all hemlock, heavily fragrant in the humid heat.

"Whew," said Jed, sitting on a mossy rock jutting out of the wall. Ulfin sat, panting, in front of them both. "Do you think he's taking us where I think he is?"

Melissa nodded reluctantly. "I only hope the hermit's not there," she said.

But Ulfin was on his feet again, urging them on, as if telling them it was important that they hurry. And they knew, remembering the times before when he had saved them from great danger, not to question him.

It certainly seemed as if there was danger now, for Ulfin soon slowed, stepping carefully on the dark-brown needles that covered the forest floor, smooth except for the lumps and bumps of animal holes, fallen twigs, and the rounded green leaves of mayflowers, now mostly past their bloom.

Finally, they came to the clearing where the small grayish-brown Keeper's House stood, built by the original Eli Dunn and most recently lived in by the present hermit; it was here that Melissa and Jed had first seen him. Ulfin pressed against their legs, telling them to stay still, as he had so often last winter, and then he ran ahead to make sure it was safe. The old tripod, the one the hermit had used for his ceremonies before he took Melissa and Jed to the root cellar, was still in the middle of the clearing in front of the small house with its loose shutters and its patchwork front door, made of many different sizes and kinds of wood nailed together every which way. In the yard around the tripod was an amazing collection of junk. Melissa remembered thinking last spring that the bits of metal and wood she'd seen sticking out of the snow must be just the tip of the iceberg, and she saw now that she'd been right. Two old lawnmowers leaned lazily against rocks; rusty car parts lined what would have been a front path, had there been one. There was most of an old tractor to one side, along with a large assortment of bedsprings, tools, kitchen utensils, and other rusty metal scraps that could have been almost anything when they were new.

There was no smoke coming from the chimney, a good sign, Melissa thought—until she realized that of course it was far too hot to have a fire, unless it was for cooking.

Ulfin ran to the front door and sniffed carefully all around it. Then he circled the house, still sniffing, and finally came running back to them, tail waving; he nosed them forward.

The door opened easily, letting out slightly cooler air.

The familiar musty smell hit Melissa as soon as they went inside, and it made her want to run out again—not so much because it was unpleasant, though it was, but because of the memories it brought back of the hermit's walking in and finding them there, then shutting them into what was almost a closet next to the fireplace in the bare room to the right of the door, then marching them blindfolded through the snow . . .

Ulfin ran into that bare room now, and then back to them, pawing them and dancing.

"That's where he wants us to go, I guess," said Jed, wiping the sweat off his forehead and following him slowly.

Melissa glanced into the only other downstairs room, the one to the left of the door, before she joined them. Everything there was as she remembered it—the straw broom next to the fireplace, the andirons, the pewter spoons, the skillet, the crane and its black pot—even the rock collection and the feathery bouquet of quill pens in the tin can hanging from the wall. There was no sign, she noticed with relief, that a cooking fire had been built in the fireplace at any time recently, and no sign of food.

"Okay," she whispered to herself, and went to join Jed.

Jed had opened the door of the little closet-room by the fireplace; Ulfin was scratching at the familiar old oak chest inside and whining. The chest, in which Jed and Melissa had found Eben Dunn's diary, was the only thing the original hermit had taken from Fours Crossing, Gran had told them, when he'd left the village for good after Eben had married Tabitha Ellison.

"Easy, boy," Jed was saying, fumbling with the lid. "Easy. I'm hurrying as fast as I can."

At last Jed got proper hold of the handle and swung the lid up.

"No robe," Melissa said uncomfortably, for the first thing

they'd seen in the chest before had been the hermit's white ceremonial robe, with the gold belt that matched Ulfin's collar.

"Wouldn't be here," Jed said, but he didn't sound very sure of himself. "He had it with him in the root cellar, remember?"

Ulfin nudged Melissa and then stared intently into one corner of the chest, as if signaling her there was something there he wanted. Melissa knelt beside him and tried to look where he was looking. "It's not this, is it, Ulfin?" she said, touching the old dagger that lay on top of the pile of books and fabric that made up the bulk of the chest's contents. "Or this?" She lifted out one of the two heavy gobletlike cups, carved with patterns of endlessly interlocking circles.

Ulfin's nose darted into the chest, under where the cup had been. Delicately, with his teeth, he picked out the smallest of the books and held it out toward Melissa till she took it from him. Then he sat down, panting, watching her.

"It's Eben's diary," said Jed, pointing to the foreign-looking cipher letters on the book's crumbling spine. He reached for it, but Ulfin pushed his hand away. "For you, I guess," he said, smiling. "I guess he knows who the cipher-solver is."

"Knows who's got the alphabet, anyway," said Melissa, laying the diary gently in her lap and putting the cup back.

Ulfin licked Melissa's hand as she reached up to close the chest, as if thanking her for taking the diary. Then he ran to the door and whined.

"We're coming, lad," said Jed. "We're coming. Melissa, let's go; he's getting pretty nervous."

Melissa, resisting the urge to look at the diary again then and there, joined him at the door.

Ulfin hurried them through the close and humid woods, beside the path this time, instead of actually on it—"as if," Jed said uneasily, "he's trying to hide from something . . ."

142

Just then Ulfin stopped, freezing, and pressed hard against Jed's legs.

Jed and Melissa froze, too, straining their ears.

Birds sang—and then stopped. There was the slightest of breezes for a moment, but it quickly faded. And then . . .

"Look," Jed mouthed soundlessly, pointing.

There was a bit of white fabric caught on a bush.

And a flash of white to the rear, moving along the path.

Melissa held her breath, too frightened even to shake.

Ulfin, except for his twitching nose, was a golden statue between them and the path; luckily, they were hidden from it by low bushes.

There was no sound of footsteps, but the flashes of white grew more frequent, came closer, and became the hermit in his white ceremonial robe, walking slowly along the path, looking to the right and left, frowning, muttering.

Melissa wondered how long she could go on holding her breath without fainting; her lungs felt ready to burst. The back of her neck itched, damp with sweat; then her shoulders; her foot began to go to sleep.

Slowly, the hermit passed.

Melissa waited a few more seconds, then allowed herself to breathe but not to move. She had no idea how long they stayed there, but they kept still even beyond the time that Ulfin pawed them, nudged them, urged them on.

"Just a minute, lad," Jed whispered. "We want to be sure."

Finally, Ulfin barked, and afraid that his barking would call the hermit back, they cautiously let him lead them forward. He went to the other side of the path this time and took them on a different route through the forest, sniffing out a rough and trackless way that forced them to stoop under low branches and dive through underbrush—but it kept them hidden, and felt safer.

They didn't speak till they came out again at the far edge of Gran's field. Melissa was glad of the sun, though it was instantly hotter without the cover of the trees.

"Good boy," said Jed, hugging Ulfin.

"We should tell the police," said Melissa. "And Rhiannon."

"The police," Jed answered. "I don't know about Rhiannon."

"Oh, Jed, come on! She should know. She's trying to help, truly."

"Do what you like," he said.

It was then that Melissa noticed how pale he was, and that his hands shook. "Do I look the way you do?" she asked softly, and at that he smiled faintly and said, "You sure do. Holy cow, was that ever a narrow one!" His smile broadened. "Maybe you'd rather go back to Boston, after all. It's bound to be safer."

"No," she said stubbornly, suddenly serious. "Less than ever. We've got to finish this. *We*. But do you believe me now that whatever's wrong is the hermit's doing, not Rhiannon's?"

Without answering, Jed reached for the diary and opened it. "Holy cow," he said again, holding it out to her. "Holy, holy cow."

Less than three months ago, when they'd first looked at the diary, Melissa and Jed had marveled at the tiny, odd-looking cipher symbols crowding its pages. Now those same pages were blank.

Plain blank paper, yellowy-brown with age.

As they looked at each other in dismay, Ulfin stiffened, a growl rumbling in his throat.

And from deep in the steamy forest, both Melissa and Jed were sure they heard the hermit laugh.

16

"All right, all right," Chief Dupres barked into his telephone. "If you order us to, Henry, then we've got to, don't we? But it's a waste of time if you ask me. Yes, I know you aren't asking me, but I'm telling you, anyway. She's just a little wisp of a thing, for heaven's sake—mass hysteria, that's what this town's got. What's more, it's ugly and I don't want any part of it—and listen, Henry, I'm not going to keep that to myself, you hear, meeting or no meeting!"

"Yes?" snapped Chief Dupres, slamming the phone down and looking up at Jed and Melissa, who had been standing quietly at his door, waiting. His phone had been busy when they'd tried to call from Gran's, relieved that she hadn't been home, for they didn't want to worry her, at least not before the police knew. "Oh, it's you," he said. "I hope this is a social call, because right now I've got more trouble than I can handle. First Alex Titus and his dad-blamed petition, asking us to arrest that poor girl and put her in jail if she won't leave town . . ."

Melissa started to interrupt, but the chief went right on talking, as if he hadn't noticed. ". . . which of course we can't do," he said, "without evidence, and anyway, she's promised to stay in touch and done it. What's more, she's brought something once or twice—cookies, yesterday." He held out a box of brownies absentmindedly; Jed and Melissa both shook their heads as politely as they could; they had never seen the chief so agitated. "And now Henry Ellison tells me he's calling a special town meeting—to try to calm the town down, *he* says—but mark my words, there'll be trouble. Too much fear, he says, with the hermit at large and everyone thinking Miss Jones let him loose; *he* thinks the meeting'll settle things—but if I know people, some folks'll call for a vigilante group, or want to set up patrols, or some fool thing like that. Even my own wife's been muttering about Miss Jones every time the milk turns sour or the hens don't lay. If I didn't know better, I'd say we were all back in the 1600s or 1700s."

"Chief Dupres . . ." Jed began.

The chief, rubbing his forehead, held up one hand, his index finger extended as if asking them to wait; Jed closed his mouth, but he looked as if it was going to be very hard for him to be patient much longer.

The chief got up and opened the small door that led into the police dispatcher's office. "Sarah," he boomed, "you got any aspirin?"

A small elderly woman in a flowery dress appeared at the door, holding out an aspirin bottle and a full glass of water, apparently having anticipated the chief's request.

"Thanks," said the chief, gulping pills.

"Hello, Jed, Melissa," said the dispatcher pointedly, as if to remind the chief they were there.

"Hello, Mrs. Goodel," said Melissa, nudging Jed, who smiled thinly.

146

"Hot, isn't it?" Sarah Goodel remarked, taking the bottle and glass back from the chief; he grunted and sat down at his desk, his head in his hands. "You'd think it was August, wouldn't you, or July, 'stead of June? Well, you must have business with the chief. Regards to your gran, Melissa."

Mrs. Goodel left, and the chief raised his head, looking a little embarrassed. "Sorry," he said gruffly. "What can I do for you?"

Melissa glanced at Jed, wondering if their news would cause another outburst. "Well," she began, "we were just—er—up in the woods . . ."

"Near the Keeper's House," supplied Jed.

"And we—we're pretty sure we saw the hermit . . ."

At that, the chief groaned loudly and seized a pad of paper and a pen. For several minutes he questioned them closely, then called in his sergeant and said, "Charley, put out an all-points; the kids think they saw the hermit up near the Keeper's House—send someone up there right away. And then I want you to stick to these two like a burr, you hear me? Anyplace they go without an adult, you go. And I'd appreciate it, you two," he said to Jed and Melissa, "if you didn't make poor Charley run all over these mountains and woods keeping up with you. You confine yourselves to the village, you hear me, at least for the next few days. Then we'll see."

"We—we've got Ulfin," said Jed. "He can take care of us."

"He's a good dog, son," said the chief, "and that's a fact, but I'd still feel better putting you under police protection. I know it's a bore, but Charley here is a pretty good sport, aren't you, Charley? Literally, too—he can even play a little baseball, right, Charley?"

"Used to play first base for the police team down to Corestown," Charley said modestly.

Jed's mouth twitched; he hadn't touched a baseball in over a year. Melissa hated organized sports.

"You go in Jed's house, or Melissa's, or a store or someplace like that, he'll stay outside. But anyplace outdoors, he'll be with you, from now on."

"Even at the graduation party?" Jed asked. "That's not allowed, really."

"By then," said the chief with determination, "we're going to have that old hermit behind bars again, you mark my words. If controlling the town after that stupid meeting doesn't take up all my time."

"When is the meeting?" asked Melissa, wondering if she and Jed would be allowed to take part in it.

"Day after tomorrow," the chief said grimly.

"Can we go up Round Top and tell Rhiannon? About the hermit? And about the meeting?"

"No, you can't!" the chief roared. "I'll tell her myself; she's due in at any minute."

"What about nights?" Jed asked. "I mean, there *are* two of us."

"Nights you'll be all right, safe and sound in your own houses, won't you? I'm not worried about that." The chief reached for his phone. "Now go along with you. I'm going to call up to Hiltonville for extra men. Dragnet the woods, that's what we'll do. We'll get him, don't you worry."

"Still," Jed whispered as they left, with Charley walking discreetly behind them like a Secret Service man, self-consciously whistling as if to show he wasn't eavesdropping, "I think I'll make extra sure Ulfin's out at night."

"He has been," Melissa whispered back. "Remember when Rhiannon said he should stay with us? He's been coming since before then and sleeping under my window. Or outside the dining-room one—I've never been sure if it's really me he's

148

guarding or the plates. I wish we could see Rhiannon," she added wistfully.

"You know what?" said Jed. "Right now, so do I."

Melissa checked that night before she went to bed, and sure enough, there was Ulfin, lying under her window in the moonlight, head up and facing out toward the woods.

She sat at her desk for a long time after Pride and Joy had purred himself to sleep, sure that she should examine the diary again more thoroughly, but feeling about it, now that its pages were blank, as she sometimes felt about her English homework: that it was a difficult chore she'd rather put off. But if Ulfin had led them to it . . .

Sighing, she took the diary out and thumbed through it, looking for some sign of the cipher letters. She'd already tacked the cipher alphabet to the wall above her desk:

ς - A	▣ - H	△ - O	♁ - V
Ɣ - B	℃ - I	< - J	⟿ - W
∧ - C	< - J	ℐ - Q	⌂ - X
☉ - D	ʃ - K	ʌ° - R	⟿ - Y
⊥ - E	⊟ - L	✕ - S	⎯ᵥ - Z
✕ - F	✓ - M	♦ - T	
↑ - G	ϒ - N	▽ - U	

For a moment she wondered if the hermit had just substituted a blank book for the diary. But then the pages wouldn't be yellow and brittle the way they were. Besides, the cipher letters on the book's crumbling reddish-brown binding were just as she remembered them.

But how, then, could the letters inside have become invisible?

Invisible—invisible ink!

But you have to write in invisible ink to begin with. You can't use it to make something visible disappear.

Except with magic, of course.

I'm as bad as Mr. Titus, she scolded herself, getting up and pacing restlessly around her room while Pride and Joy raised his head and blinked his yellow-green eyes at her reproachfully. Maybe Mr. Titus isn't so wrong after all, in general, anyway, she thought. How can I keep telling myself that there's no such thing as magic when there are so many things that can't be explained in the ordinary way?

Superstitious idiot, she scolded herself, going back to her desk. You *are* as bad as Mr. Titus.

Heat, she thought suddenly, picking up the diary again— but that's for invisible ink. Still . . .

A breeze stirred her curtains gently; she opened her window wider to let it in. Ulfin's tail twitched, acknowledging her, but he kept his eyes turned toward the field behind the house and the woods beyond. I wonder, Melissa thought wistfully, for what felt like the hundredth time, if it's going to rain—the wind seems to be rustling the leaves now . . .

Heat, she thought again. Why not try?

Quietly she put on her bathrobe and crept down the dark stairs to the kitchen. She turned on the electric stove and, careful not to scorch the book, held one page out over the largest burner.

Nothing.

She turned a few pages and tried again.

Still nothing—but . . .

She bent closer. Of course! It was as if the hermit had somehow erased the letters, and as with anything erased, a faint impression remained, barely visible when light came through the page from behind, but visible nonetheless.

It's lucky, she thought, running quietly upstairs again, that Eben Dunn wrote on only one side of each page.

Her curtains were still when she went back to her room, and

Pride and Joy was asleep again, but the rustling sound was louder and more regular, almost pattering—rain at last, she thought absently, moving her bedside lamp to her desk; maybe that will make it cooler. There was even a slight growly rumble of thunder.

The bedside lamp was better than the light from the stove, but still didn't quite work; she couldn't make out the symbols clearly enough to be sure of copying them accurately. Sighing, Melissa went downstairs again, leaving the book in her room, to get a stronger light bulb from the cupboard in the kitchen.

I hope, she thought, hearing thunder again, closer, as she passed through the dining room, that the lights don't go off in the storm. They so often do . . .

And then she froze in the door between the dining room and the kitchen, for something was moving outside against the window, silhouetted in the moonlight—something dark and tall—with another something moving against it, struggling . . .

That rumble—it wasn't thunder; it was Ulfin's growl! And there was no wind or rain. What she'd heard before was the hermit creeping around outside the window, stealthily trying to open the latch.

The plates! thought Melissa, stifling a scream. She snatched them off the wall and ran wildly from the dining room.

Where to hide them? Cellar? Her own room? Gran's room? No, that would wake Gran, maybe frighten her—as if Gran could be frightened. Henhouse? She'd have to go outside, then. Besides, she should call the police—she should help Ulfin—cellar, maybe that was best, there'd be a shovel or something down there, too, that she could use as a weapon . . .

Hold on, Ulfin, she told him silently, running down the cellar stairs in the dark, afraid to turn on a light, stumbling . . .

She thrust the plates unceremoniously under a pile of coal left over from the days when Gran didn't have oil heat, and groped around among the garden tools till she felt what seemed to be a shovel. Without stopping to make sure it was, she ran back up the stairs to call the police—but then Ulfin's snarl changed to a yelp, and without giving herself time to be afraid, she burst out the kitchen door.

"Stop right where you are!" she commanded, surprising herself—but then she saw that someone else had gotten there before her and was struggling against the hermit along with Ulfin, someone in a long cloak, ghostly in the semidarkness.

"Police," gasped Rhiannon's voice. "Melissa, call them. No —stay away! Call the police—his power is growing now— almost Midsummer—*call!*"

Melissa dropped the shovel and ran inside again, heart leaping in her chest. She found the police number taped to the phone and dialed frantically.

"Fours Crossing Police," came Sarah Goodel's voice, sleep-ily, after three rings.

"Melissa Dunn," Melissa gasped. "Come quick—the hermit —up at Gran's—oh, please, quick!" she added, for there was a muffled cry of pain—a woman's voice . . .

She dropped the phone and ran outside again to see an angry heap writhing on the ground—Rhiannon, the hermit, and Ulfin, a tangle of robes and fur and arms and legs. Some-one broke free—Rhiannon—she groped at her neck and Melissa ran forward, sobbing—was she hurt?

But Rhiannon was pulling something out of her bosom, something on a chain—it glinted in the moonlight—and the hermit, as Ulfin leaped for his throat, recoiled from it, falling back with a stifled cry, throwing up his arm to protect himself. Rhiannon held the glittering object steadily before him.

The hermit thrust Ulfin from him violently, broke free, and

vanished into the darkness, whether by running or by other means, Melissa was never sure.

Rhiannon fell to the ground; Melissa ran to her. Ulfin, apparently unhurt, followed and licked her face as soon as Melissa managed to turn her over.

Her eyes were closed, and there was blood above her breast.

"Melissa?" The back door light flashed on and Gran, deceptively frail-looking in her white summer nightgown, hurried down the steps. "Land sakes, child, what's happened—why, it's Miss Jones!"

Melissa explained as briefly as she could while Gran helped her carry Rhiannon into the house and settle her on the sofa in the living room. Ulfin followed anxiously, staying close to Rhiannon, who now opened her eyes and smiled weakly. "I— I am all right," she said as if from very far away, with great effort. "Thank you." She held out her hand and drew Ulfin to her, looking into his eyes. "Noblest of dogs," she whispered. "Go to the others. Quickly. Melissa, let him out, please."

"But . . ." began Gran—but Melissa moved swiftly, opening the door for Ulfin just as Charley and Chief Dupres, revolvers gleaming at their hips and nightsticks at the ready, burst out of the cruiser.

"Where is he?" they both said; Ulfin, unseen by everyone but Melissa, streaked toward Round Top fast as lightning.

"He got away," said Melissa. "But it's all right. He didn't . . ."

Chief Dupres put his hands on Melissa's shoulders. "You okay?" he roared. "My God, and I said nights would be safe! I should be drummed off the force!"

"Shut up, Chief," said Charley bluntly. "You're not a seer. Looks like we've got a victim in here." He went into the living room, the chief right behind him.

Rhiannon was sitting up now; the wound, Melissa saw with

relief as Gran dabbed at it with a damp cloth, was smaller than it had seemed before. "You all right, Miss Jones?" the chief asked. "What happened?"

Melissa sat quietly while Rhiannon told her part of the story, but started to protest when the chief demanded, a touch of suspicion in his voice, despite his earlier defense of Rhiannon, "What were you doing here so late at night, Miss Jones, if I might ask?"

"Walking my dog," said Rhiannon without flinching, putting her hand over Melissa's briefly, silencing her. "She seemed to want to come here, and I believe in giving animals as much freedom as possible. Besides, I thought she might be after something, maybe even the hermit."

The chief looked around the room. "And where's your dog now?" he asked.

"I sent her away when I saw the hermit," said Rhiannon quietly. "I had reason to believe the hermit might go to the root cellar if he was successful in his purpose here—if I could not prevail against him. I wanted my dog there to confront him if necessary, to hold him for you if she could. Perhaps they are both there now . . ."

"Anyone see you come here?" the chief asked gruffly.

"Not till Melissa did, that I know of."

"But you did see the hermit?" the chief asked Melissa.

"Yes," she said emphatically, still worried that the chief might be thinking it was Rhiannon who had tried to break in.

But if the chief had thought that, he seemed to have dismissed it now.

"Well," he said, "best you stay the night here, Miss Jones, if Miz Dunn will have you." Gran nodded. "And best you have Doc Ellison see to that," he added, pointing to Rhiannon's wound.

"It is only a scrape," Rhiannon said. "We had a bit of a tussle and my—my necklace scratched me."

"Ummmm," said the chief. "Charley . . ."

"You couldn't move me if you tried, Chief," Charley said cheerfully, taking off his hat and settling down in Gran's big overstuffed chair.

"I'll put a man on the Ellison house," the chief said, "though I daresay Jed and Seth between 'em can look after themselves."

"Melissa did a pretty good job of that tonight," said Rhiannon.

Melissa smiled at her gratefully.

"Now," said Chief Dupres grimly, striding toward the door, "for the hermit. Root cellar, you said, Miss Jones?"

Rhiannon nodded, and the chief stumped out.

"Well," said Gran when he'd gone, "cup of tea, Charley? Rhiannon? Melissa? Or maybe iced?"

"Iced, please," said Melissa.

Much later that night, when Gran had gone to bed and Charley was settled downstairs with a pile of old crossword puzzles and a pitcher of iced tea, Rhiannon, whom Gran had put in the guest room across from her own, knocked quietly on Melissa's door.

"Shh," she whispered, slipping inside. "You must sleep—I will not stay long. But I want you to take this. Wear it always, as long as he is uncaught and wanting the summer plate and I dare not think what else. You saw me use it; that is how you must use it, too, if he threatens you. You may not need it— but in case."

Rhiannon slipped the silver chain from her neck and over Melissa's head.

Melissa looked down at the pendant that hung from the chain, softly gleaming even in the semidarkness of her room. "But," she said, "the root cellar—won't he be there?"

"Perhaps," said Rhiannon. "But I do not think he will be caught tonight."

"Then won't you need this?" She held out the pendant, trying not to think of the hermit's coming back to Gran's.

"I have other protections," Rhiannon said softly. "You do not."

Melissa examined the pendant in the moonlight. It was circular, like the plates, only instead of just one branch of the even-sided cross, all four were there, making quadrants edged with cipher symbols, each group of symbols separated from the others by pairs of leaves. Each pair of leaves was one of the kinds on the plates: rowan, oak, hemlock, and maple.

"But," Melissa said to Rhiannon, puzzled, "I don't understand. If he *likes* the Old Ways, why doesn't he like this?"

"Because this," said Rhiannon, "shows the year as it moves from season to season, pure and strong—the year he violated by taking spring, and would violate again. Remember that the summer plate was warm, to warn us." Rhiannon bent swiftly and kissed Melissa's hair, so lightly Melissa barely felt it. "Sleep well, my daughter, and safely."

Rhiannon left the room, almost seeming to float in the moonlight, and Melissa blinked back the tears that had sprung to her eyes again at the words "My daughter." Maybe Joan Savage was right, after all.

She went back to bed and slept, her hand curled protectively around the pendant—around the unbroken year, all four seasons, in an endless, never-dying cycle.

17

For the rest of that night and all the next day, police from both Fours Crossing and Hiltonville combed the woods, but found, as Rhiannon had predicted to Melissa, no sign of the hermit. The Hiltonville police chief called his men home, and Chief Dupres, shaking his head, ordered his own men, under Charley, to keep a sharp eye on the town the night of the meeting.

The meeting was held in the school gym, where chairs had been set up. Nearly everyone in the little village was there—although Seth and Rhiannon were not—fanning themselves with copies of the town newspaper, which had put out a special edition supposedly reviewing everything known about the hermit and Rhiannon so far. But it isn't everything, Melissa thought, scanning her copy of the paper from her seat between Gran and Jed; Tommy was in the back with his parents. The people who write the paper really don't know a thing about either the hermit or Rhiannon.

There was a report of a quickly taken poll, saying that town opinion was divided about equally as to whether the hermit had been after the plates when he'd tried to break into Gran's, or after Melissa.

And, worse, whether Rhiannon had been there to stop him or there as his accomplice.

But despite everything Melissa and Jed had tried to explain at the trial, there was nothing about the Old Ways and the New, nothing about the battle that was really going on. Melissa found herself wondering, as she watched people file into the gym, if anyone in Fours Crossing besides her and Jed would ever really understand—not that we do completely, either, she thought, trying to be fair; not that we've always believed even when we understood.

At eight o'clock sharp, Mr.-Henry-Ellison-the-Selectman strode regally to the front of the room, where a small portable speaker's podium had been set up, and rapped on it sharply for attention.

"I'm glad to see so many of you turned out tonight," he said without formal introduction. He smiled. "In fact, so many of you are here that I hope all the watchdogs in town are extra-alert tonight—and I hope," he said more seriously after the chuckle had died away, "that you all locked your doors and windows before you came here. If any of you didn't, I suggest you either go do it now or give your names to Charley, who'll have it seen to."

One or two people quietly left their seats.

"Now then." Mr. Ellison consulted a piece of paper he had laid on the podium in front of him. "There's no precedent for this kind of meeting, Mrs. Titus tells me. I'm going to run it myself, since I called it, with apologies to the town moderator." Here he nodded to an elderly man in the front row, who smiled and nodded back. "And I'm not going to run it in the usual way, because we don't have a whole list of things to discuss, only one. What I am going to do is ask Mr. Titus, who as you all know is the one who started the petition going around, to get up and explain to you what he thinks should be done, and then I'll accept comments from the floor." He looked out over the podium at the villagers. "Comments from the floor in an *orderly* fashion," he said. "One by one. Hands raised and no shouting. Feeling runs high about this, I know. But we won't get anything decided if we get too emotional. Now then, Alex."

There was some whispering while Mr. Ellison moved aside and Mr. Titus got up and went to the front of the room. He was wearing a suit, Melissa noticed with surprise, realizing she'd rarely seen a Fours Crossing man—with the exception of Dr. Ellison, who was the local physician, Mr. Savage, and, on special occasions, Henry Ellison—wear one.

Mr. Titus put a large sheaf of papers down on the podium, cleared his throat nervously, and blinked out at the audience, his glasses low on his nose.

"Friends," he said. Then he cleared his throat once more and began again. "Friends. I don't have to tell you I'm not used to—er—public speaking. Last time I got up on my hind legs and said anything in town meeting was twenty years ago, when there was all that fuss about puttin' a big road through the green. 'Member that?"

There was an affirmative murmur from the crowd.

"Well, those of you who do also remember that I was agin it like most of you were, because it'd ruin the town. Bring business here, folks that was for it said, but we all knew we didn't need outsiders here, with ice cream shops and filling stations and hamburger stands, and candy wrappers strewn all over the place for poor Frank Grange and his boys to pick up.

"Seems to me, same thing's happening now, only different. Now, I'm as friendly as the next fellow . . ." (Here Melissa saw Gran cover her mouth with her hand.) ". . . but outsiders are as outsiders do. And we've had nothing but trouble since that woman come here. Now, I'm not one for accusations. But there's such a thing as a disruptive influence, and I say that's what we've got here. Restless children, singing witch rhymes in the street. It's bad enough, the weather being unseasonably hot"—he wiped his brow, as if for effect—"and the crops withering and good Fours Crossing dirt blowing away. But we've got a dangerous criminal at large now, too. And it's no secret, you all know it, that the Jones woman—or whatever her name really is—came here to see him, went every day up to Hiltonville to see him, saying he was some kind of relative. Many of you saw 'em go off early in the morning, her'n Seth Ellison, and come back late at night . . ." He scanned the room as if looking for someone and then added, ". . . Seth all restless and bothered, like a man bewitched . . ."

Gran, who had been twitching in her seat, suddenly jumped up. "Oh, for heaven's sake, Alex, you do run on! Land sakes, don't you have the brain to recognize when a body's lovesick?"

Mr. Ellison stepped rapidly to the podium and rapped for order. "Mrs. Dunn," he said, his eyes twinkling despite the stern look on his face, "you're out of order, ma'am, I'm sorry to say. Your turn'll come. Let Alex have his say."

Gran sat down, muttering.

"Someone," Mr. Ellison said, looking over the heads of the crowd, "open that door in the back. We're going to need all the *cool* air we can get."

Mr. Titus glared at him and spoke over the restrained titter that followed. ". . . like a man bewitched, I was saying," he repeated insistently. "Now, there's nothing wrong with that— it's not my place or anyone's to criticize what a man does in his spare time or who he sees—even if that man does have a motherless boy to look after . . ."

160

Gran put her hand on Jed's; he'd made a move as if to stand up.

". . . no, that kind of thing is none of our affair—as I'd have said if I'd had a chance before Miz Dunn got all emotional. What *is* our affair, friends, is the *fact* that the hermit is at large again, the *fact* that he is a kidnapper, the *fact* that this Rhiannon Jones or whatever she calls herself was the last person to see him before he—er—escaped."

There was a murmur of approval, but over it came Mr. Savage's voice, interrupting: "And another *fact*, Alex Titus, is that as far as anyone in this room knows, you have no license to practice law and no training in police work . . ."

"Jonathan," said Henry Ellison to Mr. Savage, "Jonathan, you're out of order."

"This whole meeting's out of order," said Mr. Savage angrily, striding to the podium.

Joan, Melissa noticed, looked very pink and very proud.

Mr. Titus pulled out a white handkerchief and polished his glasses. Then he wiped his brow and looked nervously at Mr. Ellison, who moved forward, but not in any hurry that Melissa could see.

"The *fact*," Mr. Savage continued quickly, "is that what Alex here is doing is trying to put together a lot of loosely connected bits of circumstantial evidence to accuse and possibly in effect convict in your minds a young woman whose most grievous fault as far as I can see is that she wasn't born and brought up in Fours Crossing. Anyone who listens to such drivel should be ashamed. Anyone who *thinks* that way should be ashamed. I don't imagine for a minute that Bradford Ellison's idea when he brought religion to this village was to close it to strangers . . ."

Mr. Ellison by now was standing next to Mr. Savage. "Jonathan," he said quietly, putting his hand on Mr. Savage's shoulder, "the fact also is that you're still out of order. I'd truly hate to have to throw you out. You'll get your turn."

"Sorry, Henry," Mr. Savage muttered. "But some things have to be argued down before they do irrevocable harm." Mr. Savage went back to his seat.

Mr. Titus wiped his brow again.

"No one is asking for any kind of conviction," he said smoothly. "No one is making definite accusations. I'm just asking what I know you're all thinking: don't we have a right to request someone to leave our town when they seem to be causing it trouble?"

Mr. Ellison stood again, but Mr. Titus held up his hand, saying, "Now, just one more thing before I sit down. I'm going to ask one of the children to come up here. Susie Coffin . . ."

"Oh, holy cow," said Jed under his breath in disgust. "She's just a baby."

Little Susie Coffin, who nearly three months earlier had led the Spring Festival procession, came to the front of the room in a frilly pink dress and wearing pink bows in her blond hair.

"Mrs. Coffin certainly dressed her all up," Gran said disapprovingly. "You'd think she'd be against this—this foolishness."

"Now, Susie," said Mr. Titus, kneeling down to her level, "will you sing your song for all the people? Your jump-rope song? Just the way you sang it for me?"

Susie put her head on one side coyly.

"Come on, Susie."

Very softly, Susie began: "Witchy, witchy, witchy."

"That's fine, Susie, that's very nice. A little louder now."

"Dear God," said Gran, closing her eyes. "Someone stop this."

"Witchy, witchy, witchy," Susie sang louder. "Twitchy, twitchy, twitchy. Twitch a witch, witch a twitch." She began to giggle. "Her name is Rhi-an-non!" Susie ran back to her seat in gales of self-conscious laughter.

For a moment, no one in the room moved.

"Maybe Mr. Titus just dug his own grave, Miz Dunn," Jed whispered. "I don't think anyone liked that much."

Melissa looked at him. She hadn't been sure just which side he'd come down on at the meeting.

He turned and smiled at her. "You should know," he whispered, "that I come through in the end. The way I see it, Rhiannon saved you from the hermit."

Melissa felt warmth spread through her, and she squeezed his hand impulsively. He got very red, and she took her hand quickly away.

"Now," Mr. Titus was saying, "what could be more eloquent than that? Out of the mouths of babes . . ."

Mr. Savage had leapt to his feet almost before Mr. Ellison called for comments from the floor.

"Out of the mouths of babes," he said, "come words fit for babes, with the imperfect understanding of babes behind them." He glared at Mr. Titus, who had sat down smugly beside his embarrassed-looking wife. "Only a desperate man very unsure of his grounds, it seems to me, would use a children's jump-rope rhyme to reinforce his 'facts.' If I didn't believe it would be exploitation, I would ask little Susie what that rhyme means and who it's about and why it's sung. But all of you know as well as I do what her answer would be. *That child is six years old,* Alex Titus, and she knows not what she says."

Mr. Savage faced the crowd. "Ladies and gentlemen," he said, his face growing shiny with the heat as he talked, "I have been proud all my life to be a Fours Crossing man. I am

163

on the verge right now of not being proud. I ask you to come to your senses, to be the reasonable people I know you truly are. We have come through a bad winter, a devastating flood. We have been rocked by a kidnapping and a trial, and now the escape of a convicted criminal, judged to be insane, who we have reason to believe may be in the area. The weather's unseasonably hot; we're worried about our crops. But let's not, like people hundreds of years ago who knew no better, heap all our ills on the back of an innocent scapegoat and send her unjustly out into the wilderness. Let us face our troubles squarely, analyze them one by one, and solve our problems like intelligent twentieth-century human beings."

There was a smattering of applause when Mr. Savage sat down—but there was also quite a lot of angry muttering. A man Melissa didn't know raised his hand.

"Ephraim?" said Mr. Ellison. "Go ahead."

"Well, I dunno," said the man called Ephraim, scratching his head. "I'm sure Jonathan Savage's right about a lot of things. He knows more'n we do about the law, and that's another of those facts seems we're all so proud of. But I know what I see, and so do all of you. Won't do any harm, seems to me, to ask that young woman to leave. Just to be on the safe side, like. We can be polite about it, no reason not to be. I don't know as we'll have to say much about jail. Chances are she'll leave when we ask; most folks would, anyway. And if she does, well, mebbe the hermit will, too. Says she's his relative, after all. Mebbe they'll both go back where they came from . . ."

"Ephraim," Gran called out. "Eli John Dunn's lived here as long as you!"

"Well, yes, Janet," the man said. "In a manner of speaking. But I dunno. He's a strange one, no mistake. After all, he's spent most of his life in the woods behind your place in that old Keeper's House. Wouldn't hurt if he'd leave. Mebbe then we could all get back to normal." Somewhat uncertainly, the man called Ephraim sat down.

Mr. Ellison recognized a woman.

"Listen," she said, "I don't know much about the law. And I'm enough of a product of the twentieth century to know that the weather's caused by—well, by whatever it *is* caused by. I think we should put the things together that go together. I agree with Mr. Savage there. But I'm a mother. And I'd like to appeal to all of you who are also mothers—and fathers. I know Mr. Ellison said we weren't to get—well, emotional. But I'm not ashamed to get emotional when it comes to my children. The *fact*, Mr. Savage, is that there's a dangerous kidnapper on the loose. And the fact is, however much it's circumstantial, that this Rhiannon Jones has some connection to him. It's true we don't really know what the connection is. But I won't rest at night till I know she's gone and him with her. What I think we should do is form a town committee and go to her and ask her where he is. And ask her to turn him over to the authorities. And then ask her to leave."

There was a burst of applause, and then Melissa felt her own hand go up. It was as if it moved of its own accord, without her thought or will behind it.

"Melissa Dunn?" said Mr. Ellison.

Words crowded out Melissa's nervousness. "Rhiannon's trying to *help*," she said. "I—I know her—well, better than most of you. She's a good, kind person, truly she is. Why . . ." She looked around, searching the room for Tommy. "She saved Tommy Coffin from the flood. And she saved lots of animals, too. She helped fill sandbags. She wanted to help clean up after the flood—it's not her fault that she didn't know when to go. She's been at my gran's for tea and—well, Gran says she's fine. But that's not the point. The point is that even

165

though she's some kind of relative of the hermit's, she—she knows better than anyone that he's—well, bad, I guess you could call it. Look, I'm a relative of his, too, and he kidnapped me. Rhiannon's trying to protect us from him. Really—the other night when—when the hermit tried to get into our house, Rhiannon tried to stop him . . ."

Mr. Titus got up. "You don't know that, child!" he shouted. "You only know she was there. She could've been with him. I say she was."

Someone else shouted, "Stands to reason she was! She's always been around when there's trouble."

"She was fighting with him," Melissa said angrily. "I *saw* her. Gran saw her, too, at least right after . . ."

"I say the girl's right," came Chief Dupres's voice. "Least the woman had a wound on her to prove it. And she sure didn't act like a conspirator. I'm convinced she's not harboring him—doesn't know where he is any more'n the rest of us do."

"Lots of folks don't act like what they are," Mr. Titus shouted back. "Look at where she lives—up in that shack on Round Top, not like decent folks. Plays moony foreign songs on an old harp, I'm told, keeps a goat and a sparrow hawk, goes around in some cape or other; weird, like that black robe the hermit wore at the trial. Up to no good . . ."

"Oh, please!" Melissa shouted above the crowd, half of whom were on their feet, and above Mr. Ellison, who was helplessly calling for order. "Please *listen!* She's truly helping. There's danger, she says, from the hermit . . ."

"If this room doesn't quiet down immediately," Mr. Ellison boomed, cupping his hands to form a megaphone, "I am going to call on the police to clear it."

Angrily, noisily, people sat down.

"Now," said Mr. Ellison, "it may be premature, but I'm

going to call for a vote before things get any further out of hand. May I remind you that this meeting has the power only to suggest, not to act with any true authority? The Board of Selectmen will take under advisement . . ."

"Ha!" said Mr. Titus angrily. "Listen to that! You know whose side he's on, don't you?"

"Mr. Titus," said Mr. Ellison, looking very tall, "kindly bear in mind what I said about asking the police to clear the room. They can clear it of one person even more easily than of many. Now," he said, turning again to the crowd, "I want all of you who are in favor of the Selectmen's asking Miss Jones to leave town to raise your hands, bearing in mind that it will be a suggestion merely. As I understand it, we have no legal means of forcing her to leave, or of jailing her. She has not been charged with any crime . . ."

"Letting someone out of jail's a crime in my book," someone shouted.

"In anyone's," Mr. Ellison answered. "But no one's charged her with that formally and there's no real evidence that she did it."

"What do you need for evidence?" someone else shouted.

"Enough," Mr. Ellison snapped. "The discussion's closed. Show of hands, now, please. All in favor."

"Can we vote?" Melissa asked Jed as hands shot up—too many, she thought, in panic.

Jed shook his head. "We're supposed to be too young," he said, making a face. "We can speak, though—the way you did. You were great."

"No one paid any attention," she whispered back, but she was pleased at his praise nonetheless.

"Opposed?"

Melissa nudged Gran unnecessarily.

"Oh, holy cow!" Jed breathed as the room fairly blossomed

with raised and waving hands. "Melissa, look—look, it's okay! It'll be okay!"

It was okay: 75 for asking Rhiannon to leave. And a wonderful 247 against. Tommy, Melissa saw, was waving his clasped hands in triumph from the back of the room.

But when she left with Gran and Jed, Melissa saw Mr. Titus gathering a crowd of angry men around him.

18

"Why weren't you there?" Melissa asked Rhiannon on Round Top Sunday, telling her about the meeting while Charley read a newspaper some distance away, his back to them.

"They couldn't have talked freely if I had been."

Melissa rubbed Linnet's silky ears. "I'm worried about those men," she said. "The ones I saw with Mr. Titus afterward. I think maybe you should leave, anyway."

"I cannot leave," Rhiannon said gently, "until it is over. It will be soon, I feel it. It is almost Midsummer."

"Graduation," Melissa said. "Jed's rehearsing right now. There's this party the night before, he said. A bonfire and a picnic, partway up Round Top. And then he said we all march through the village in a sort of parade. It sounds like fun— Rhiannon?"

Rhiannon was staring at her. "On Midsummer Eve," she whispered, "a bonfire?"

Melissa nodded, suddenly uncomfortable. "Yes," she said. "It—it's supposed to be an old tradition in Fours Crossing." She laughed nervously, the history book fragment popping unaccountably into her head. "I don't know what 'old' means in Fours Crossing anymore," she said. "The only traditional bonfire I ever heard of here was at something called Beltane, and that must have been before there was such a thing as graduation."

"It was," Rhiannon said softly. "Bonfires for both," she said, almost as if to herself, "in many of our places—Beltane and Midsummer." She turned to Melissa. "They are both Old Times of power and celebration. I suppose a graduation is similar, yes?"

Melissa nodded, and then Rhiannon put her hands on Melissa's shoulders and asked urgently, "Will you go? Melissa, will you be there?"

Melissa nodded again, her uneasiness growing. "The Sevens go, yes. To the picnic, and after, for the marching. Alone, with no adults. The procession ends up at the school steps, Jed told me. The Eights sort of give the school to the Sevens. You know, symbolically. Why?"

Rhiannon, after a glance at Charley, who was still out of earshot, reading, reached out and touched the silver chain around Melissa's neck; the circle pendant hung inside her shirt. "Do not take this off," she said. "And be watchful." She put a hand on each side of Linnet's gentle face and looked for a long moment into her eyes. Then she smiled at Melissa. "When you go," she said, "take Linnet. I will send her to you as you climb Round Top. Do not leave her side. No—do not question me. But be watchful, my daughter. I will be nearby. Remember. When does the picnic start?"

"I don't know exactly. Twilight, I think. Suppertime. Everyone goes back down to the village when it's really dark."

"Then I will send Linnet before nightfall. Melissa, do not go into the woods on Midsummer Eve. Stay at home during the day."

Melissa shivered involuntarily. Rhiannon, giving her a swift, sympathetic glance, picked up her small harp, and played. Melissa saw nothing this time, and the music calmed her fear; she left Round Top filled with quiet strength.

That night, the night before Midsummer Eve, Melissa pored over the diary again, laboriously shining a strong light through each page, trying to read and copy down the symbols. At first she could make out only fragments of symbols, and only a few complete words, so widely separated that they told her nothing. But when she got beyond the place where the pages she had deciphered had slipped out, the impressions were clearer, stronger.

She got those pages out now, the ones she had deciphered before, and read them through again as a review. She had to supply the punctuation, for there was none in the original.

January 30

It is with a heavie Hand and sore that I, Eben Dunn, take up my Pen to commence this sad Account. I know not why I feel this premonition of Evill, but it is so strong that I feel I must fix this Account, what ever it may tell, in the Old Letters, so that only our Familie may read it.

For now, I knowe not what ails my poor Father, Eli Dunn, and it is for Feare of him that I write this and record his strange Wayes. He is spendyng a bleake and barren Wynter again I feare, still self exiled in the house he built by the Saw Mill, the sadder in that Tabitha and I are snugge and joyous in the Village, as joyous as is possible with this dark Dread that fills me unto Pannick. It is true that Loneliness suits my Father. As Leader both in civil Matters and in the Ceremonies, it was of course long his Lot to be aloof. It is not that. It is the Bitterness that I see growe in him, the Pain that seems to fill him more and more. He murmurs of

Betrayal, and he has still not permitted my Tabitha to cross the Thresh hold of his House. The last time we try'd to visit him, he threw a Stone at her Dogg, the pup I gave her from my Father's dog's own Litter, grazing our Dog's Shoulder painfully and bringing tears to my dear Tabitha's Eyes. Our poor Ulfin. He is the gentlest of Beastes . . ."

There followed a few pages about daily life—about how happy Eben was to be married to Tabitha Ellison, and about their plans for adding to their house, which of course was now Gran's house. Then another more substantial entry, the second page of which was significant now:

May 3, continued

". . . from the Forest of Winter," my poor demented Father shouted at us all, assembl'd there as we were in the Grove's Temple. And then tho it pain me sore to say it he rais'd the Circlet as a Weapon, to strike me, his Son . . .

"Circlet," Melissa knew, was what both Eben Dunn and the hermit had called the spring plate—and Eli Dunn, Eben's father, Jed and Melissa had learned from the diary, had stolen the spring plate, too, just as his descendant, their hermit, had done.

. . . Had not the blessed Dogg thrust himself between us, clattering the Circlet to the stoney floor, I know not what would have been my Fate, nor if I ever again should have held my sweet Tabitha in my Armes.

It is then that my Father, knock'd also to the Floor and reeling, grop'd his way from stone to stone like some Prehistoric Worme, some mythic Dragon, some Phoenix born of Death. For then, before our Eyes, I swear it, he mouth'd weakly Wordes that seem'd to say I will return and then, on a sudden strengthened, and whirling round, he . . .

Melissa closed her eyes; she hadn't read the diary since she and Jed had been rescued from the present-day hermit's root cellar. But the similarity struck her again between what had happened to Eben and Tabitha Dunn in 1725 and what had happened to her and to Jed a few weeks ago. Just before they'd been rescued, their hermit had lifted the plate as if it were a weapon, too; Ulfin had intervened, and the hermit had whirled and somehow vanished from the root cellar. And later, when the police had caught him, he had said exactly the same words: "I will return."

And he has, Melissa thought, shuddering.

Beltane, she thought suddenly, opening her eyes to look for the passage she had copied from the town history book, leaving blanks for the words she couldn't read:

... and the _____ burned and crackled with great vehemence this Beltane of 1725, and there were those who said it was because it was so late ...

Jed had said Beltane was on the first of May, Melissa remembered—and here it said it was "so late." As late as the third, maybe, the date of the diary entry she'd just read? Perhaps—but surely not as late as June, not as late as Midsummer, despite the connection Rhiannon had seemed to be trying to make.

... And we encased him in wicker, as of Old, and the wicker _____ and him with it and though his voice rose horribly saying, "I will return," his power could not arrest the _____. Thus vanished forever the wicked false priest and his evil pagan ways, and all of Fours Crossing rejoiced and gave thanks unto the Lord ...

"Fire," Melissa wrote carefully in the first blank, and "burned" in the second, then "fire" again.

Or "flames," she thought, trying not to let her feelings surface. It could be that, too.

I will return, she thought. Does that mean "vanished forever" was—is—untrue?

Are the two hermits the same person?

She went to the window and looked down for reassurance at Ulfin. You're being silly, she told herself. Be sensible. It's long past Beltane, and the book didn't say anything about Midsummer. And the hermit can't be the same person. He's still what he always was: a crazy old man who *thinks* he's the first Eli Dunn, who's acting out a story he's read . . .

Reluctantly, Melissa went back to her desk and the rest of the diary.

At first she could make out only isolated words: ⟨cipher⟩, that was harmless enough: May 4 with the number in Roman numerals. That was the day after Eben's last entry, so nothing was missing. Then ⟨cipher⟩—that was Beltane. And ⟨cipher⟩—delay'd. Then ⟨cipher⟩—Ulfin; ⟨cipher⟩—another dogge; ⟨cipher⟩—wicker; ⟨cipher⟩—consum'd. Then what looked like ⟨cipher⟩—O my father.

It seemed to tally, so far, fragmentary as it was, with what the history book said.

And then again ⟨cipher⟩—I will return.

With growing uneasiness, she turned the pages, looking for more. Eben seemed to have been more relaxed after his May 4 entry—his pen left less of an impression and the cipher became nearly impossible to read. But then, at the very end, which seemed to have been written years later, the impressions deepened, and Melissa bent forward intently, copying down cipher letters as fast as she could and then writing their

174

alphabet equivalents above them, till finally she had this brief outcry, the diary's final words:

And to some Dunn as yet unborne Who finds and reads this I say Welcome, and Caution. The Spirit of my Father is uneasie and in its unease will turn I fear to Evill. But none-theless—I knowe this now—he is right that the Old Wayes have been betray'd. There is some Good in them, O my Descendant, you Who are so far in the Future that I cannot see you. There is some Value in the Old Wayes for they speake of the constant, undying Things—the Seasons, the living Beastes and Trees, the timeless Thinges that join us all, the Dead with the Living, the Living with the Dead, Age after Age after Age.

Heed this, and teach it, and let my Father rest!

Melissa sat, unmoving, unseeing, those words before her, thinking with brief pain of her mother and then of Rhiannon. At last, her hands touching the silver pendant and her eyes drawn to the window and to the nearly full moon outside, she whispered, "Yes. Yes, Eben, I will heed."

19

On Midsummer Eve, short night before the year's longest day, Gran walked with Melissa down to the village, where she was to meet Tommy and Joan. In spite of the heat, there was no haze; stars dotted a clear sky, and the moon dappled the river with silver.

"It's almost as if you lived here, lambie, isn't it?" said Gran as they approached the bridge.

"I feel as if I do," said Melissa. "Much more than I ever felt I lived in Boston. Oh, Gran! I wish I could stay here forever!"

"Do you, lambie? I'd be glad to have you, both you and your daddy. But there's not much work for your daddy to do here, though I wish there were. I expect he'd get a mite bored here, the way he did when he was a young man, and left."

"How old was he when he left?" Melissa asked curiously. They were at the bridge now, sturdily rebuilt by Seth and his crew, and Melissa leaned over, looking down into the dark river water, remembering how it had surged and swirled during the flood—and how still it had been for so long before that, when it was frozen.

"Oh, not much older than Jed," Gran answered.

Melissa hesitated, then asked, "Is that why you were so upset at the idea of Jed's running away?"

Gran smiled. "Partly, I suppose. Though your daddy *was* older. No, it was more that I don't think Jed's ready to be out on his own, no matter how grown up he seems. And I'd like to see him and Seth come to terms so they'll both be at peace when he does leave."

"I wonder," said Melissa, "if they'll ever come to terms."

"If they don't," Gran said flatly, "there'll always be something missing for both of them." She patted Melissa's shoulder. "But they're on their way, I think. 'Twas just this latest business slowed them down."

"Rhiannon?"

Gran nodded. "I think Jed's sorting that out now, though. Seth, too—I don't think he's seeing her as much."

"She'll be leaving soon, I guess," Melissa said carefully, fingering the pendant under her blouse. "Gran," she asked on a sudden impulse, "where does the custom come from— the graduation one, I mean?"

"Land sakes, lambie," said Gran, "I don't know."

"What about Beltane?" Melissa asked. "Or Midsummer? Rhiannon says there used to be bonfires for both, in some places."

Gran looked a little surprised. "Well, maybe so," she said. "Yes, I think perhaps she's right." She chuckled. "It's been a long time since I heard anyone mention those old festivals, though your grandfather—and his father, too—used to talk about them." She gave Melissa a quick hug. "Shows you're a real Dunn," she said, "if you're interested in these things. Odd, though, your daddy's not, at least not that he's ever said. I suppose it's as I said about Spring Festival, Melissa. Some customs are so old no one really remembers how they began."

"But that's sad, isn't it?" Melissa said, with an intensity that surprised even herself. "I mean, if no one remembers, then no one—no one has any real *beginnings*, do they?" She thought of the hermit's anguished outcry at the trial: "It is the village, the village that is ill"—but then thought, too, of Rhiannon's warning that the hermit would try to force a return to the past, and then of Eben's words about heeding "timeless Thinges."

But who is right, she asked silently, unable to choose one; Rhiannon, who is right?

"It *is* sad," Gran was saying in answer to the question Melissa had by now almost forgotten asking, "sad when people don't remember how things began. But people go on, Melissa, and ideas change—usually"—she smiled—"for the better. Now," Gran said, giving Melissa a little pat, "come along, child, you'll be late!" She smiled again. "You look so nice, lambie! Prettiest girl there, I should think!"

Melissa felt herself blush, despite her serious mood. She did feel a little special wearing a skirt—a soft yellow one, sprigged with tiny dark-blue flowers. She'd originally planned to wear jeans, the way everyone did most days in Fours Crossing, but luckily Joan had told her she'd heard the girls usually wore skirts for the graduation party, even if it was halfway up a mountain.

"I bet even Jed'll take notice," Gran teased, her blue-green eyes twinkling.

"Oh, Gran," Melissa said, blushing deeper. "Jed's just a friend."

"Best way to start," Gran said cheerfully. "Now come along, child, do."

The Eights, Joan told Melissa, had gone on ahead, as always, to build the bonfire.

"They've got special things to do," said Tommy quietly. He seemed subdued; of course, Melissa thought, he's missing Jed already—and so am I, she realized then.

"That's what they *say*," Joan said, switching a huge picnic basket from her right arm to her left. "I think it's just that they get the fire ready and practice their songs and stuff. It's nothing mysterious, at least I don't think it is. Not like Spring Festival or anything."

"But usually earlier," said Melissa, growing suddenly nervous, "right?"

Joan nodded. "Just about three weeks earlier," she said. "Beginning of June. I like your skirt, Melissa."

"Thank you. I like yours, too," Melissa said politely. Joan's skirt was bright red, with a vivid green belt that defied the thickness of her waist, as if saying, "Well, so what if I'm around a middle that's wider than most people's? I like it!"

"Girls!" exclaimed Tommy, but without his usual spirit.

"You look pretty good yourself, Tom," Melissa said, trying to cheer him up. "White shirt, clean pants. And no green hat, either."

"It's in those mothballs," said Tommy gloomily.

"What a night!" Joan said, throwing back her head and looking up at the stars—and they walked on in silence for a while, heading toward Round Top.

Maybe I'm wrong, Melissa told herself, trying to enjoy the night as Joan was so clearly doing; maybe Rhiannon's wrong and nothing's going to happen.

But she was glad all the same that Chief Dupres had told her and Jed privately that he was breaking with tradition by stationing two men on Round Top within shouting distance of the fire, and gladder still that she had Rhiannon's pendant safe around her neck. She wondered if Rhiannon really would send Linnet to her, and when—and just as she thought it, as if wondering had summoned her, Linnet came out of the underbrush, thrusting her blunt nose into Melissa's hand, licking it, and wagging her back end in her usual tight circles. Melissa wasn't sure, but she thought she saw the flash of Dian's tail up ahead, as the moon caught a white spot.

"What a sweet dog! Whose is she, Melissa?" asked Joan, putting the basket down to pat her.

"She's Rhiannon's," said Tommy, more himself now that the dog was there. "Her name is Linnet." He reached for the basket. "My turn," he said, hefting it. "Good grief, Joanie, what's in here?"

"Cookies," Joan said. "Sandwiches: ham, bologna, egg, peanut butter, cheese. Chocolate cake. Root beer."

"I hear they're going to have *real* beer," said Tommy.

"They are not!" said Joan. "No one would let them."

"Who said anything about letting?" said Tommy. "Really. I heard a couple of the Eights talking about it."

"They couldn't *get* beer," said Joan scornfully.

"Oh, no? There are ways."

"What ways?"

They were walking more briskly now, Melissa and Linnet in the lead, and Joan and Tommy coming up behind, arguing, with the picnic basket now slung between them.

"I heard that one of the Eights met this guy who said he'd get them beer, that's all."

"Not Jed's father?" Melissa asked anxiously over her shoulder.

Tommy shook his head. "I don't think so. An old guy, someone said."

A chill swept suddenly over Melissa. But it couldn't be, she thought. He wouldn't come out of hiding. And even if he did, there'd be no reason . . .

"Listen!" said Tommy suddenly.

From the distance came a faint sound of voices singing soft, sad songs—goodbye songs, Melissa thought, goodbye to Fours Crossing, and to us . . .

"When they start the school song," Joan said, "we're supposed to answer."

"Where are the others?" Melissa asked. "The other Sevens?"

Tommy shrugged. "I think it's supposed to be like this—arriving in little groups, a few at a time." He looked at his watch. "We must be just about the last," he said. "It's late. Come on, we better hurry. And listen! There's the school song."

Joan was the first of them to join in, her high sweet voice answering the distant Eights. Melissa and Tommy followed—and Linnet, her head cocked and her bright eyes shining, looked as if she'd sing, too, if she could.

Then Melissa smelled woodsmoke, and a moment later saw the bright orange glow of a bonfire—smaller than she'd expected—but as soon as they came into view, eighth-graders began feeding the fire oak logs from a huge pile that lay nearby, and the flames leaped higher, till they seemed to reach all the way up Round Top.

Jed left the other shadowy faces surrounding the leaping flames and went to Melissa. Tommy turned away.

Melissa sensed that Jed felt a little strange, too, out at night all dressed up.

He stood in front of her, smiling. "Hi," he said. "Hey, you look nice."

"You, too." She smiled back, and if either of them blushed, neither the moonlight nor the firelight was bright enough to show it.

"It's pretty," Melissa said, nodding toward the fire. There was no sign of Chief Dupres's men; they must really be only within shouting distance, Melissa thought. "The singing's nice," she said. "We heard it on the way."

"You're supposed to," Jed said. "I remember from last year." He began leading her toward the fire, but Melissa stopped him. "There's a funny smell," she said, frowning.

Jed looked suddenly uncomfortable. "Is there?" he said vaguely. "Come on."

But Melissa caught a darkish gleam near the fire, flame-light dancing off rounded surfaces as two or three Eights lifted dark bottles to their mouths.

"It's true, then?" she asked Jed. "Beer?"

He nodded, making light of it, and moved toward the fire.

But again she stopped him, and her pendant felt warm under her blouse. "Jed," she asked, "who brought it?"

"I don't know," he said evasively. "Not Dad, anyway. That's all I care about."

"Tommy said some old man," Melissa persisted. "Who? Do—do you know him?"

Jed's face clouded. "Melissa, I don't know," he said, sounding on the edge of anger. "I know what you're thinking. But we couldn't really see him. He just stepped out of the woods with all those cases, saying nothing, and left. I don't think anyone even paid him—and I don't know who he was."

"Come on, Jed, you'd know *him!* Was it him?"

"No. At least—oh, Melissa, I don't know! What difference does it make, anyway? It's only beer."

"*Only* beer," she said, angry herself now. "After your father . . ."

"My father drinks whiskey, not beer," he said coldly. "It's not the same thing. Whiskey's stronger. Beer's okay. Come on," he said, almost wheedling, unlike himself. "Have some. It's good once you get used to it."

"So you've already had some?"

"Sure," he said, swaggering a little. "And I'm going to have some more. It's graduation, for Pete's sake. And we're going to be in high school next year. It's time we learned how to drink, even if you Sevens don't. We're not kids anymore, we're . . ."

Melissa broke away from him and ran into the shadows, but Linnet blocked her path, growling softly.

Melissa fell to her knees and buried her face in Linnet's fur, sobbing. "He'll be no good, Linnet," she whispered. "No good tonight if—if anything happens."

Linnet licked the tears from Melissa's face and grunted softly.

"Melissa?"

It was Joan, coming toward her.

Melissa dried her eyes on Linnet's willing ears and stood up, smoothing her skirt.

"There you are," Joan said cheerfully. "We're about to eat. Guess what? The Eights brought hot dogs, and we've got long sticks to roast them with." She held something out to Melissa. "Here, I brought you a beer." She giggled, holding another up in her other hand. "It's my first one ever," she said. "But I think I like it. Tastes a little funny at first, but you get used to it. Melissa?"

Melissa turned away, Linnet instantly with her.

It wasn't that she didn't approve, she knew, although she also knew that's what they all would think—she didn't know if she approved or not. Gran wouldn't, she knew that. Part of her wanted to taste it, to see what it was like. But the other part knew she had to stay alert. And she didn't trust it. Even though it was in bottles, who was to say if he'd done something to it?

If it was he.

But it couldn't be anyone else.

"Hey, Melissa!"

This time it was Tommy, jiggling her arm.

"Come on! We're going to start eating. And then there'll be the march. You don't want to be left all alone up here on Round Top, do you?" He leaned closer to her, leering, raising his arms like an imitation monster. "Ghosts'll get youuuuu . . ."

Melissa let herself be led back to the fire, Linnet again by her side. Someone thrust a hot dog into her hand, and threw a bunless one to Linnet. Someone else handed Melissa a piece of Joan's chocolate cake. People munched and reminisced, told jokes and laughed. "Do you remember," said one eighth-grader, "the time Jed Ellison fell off the swing in third grade and we all thought he was dead till he stuck out his tongue at us?"

Everyone laughed, and at last Melissa found herself joining in.

"Did you really?" she asked Jed, who had come to sit beside her.

He grinned. "Yep. Kept my eyes closed, too, and stopped breathing. Here, have a swig."

She took the bottle without thinking and swallowed. It wasn't as bad as she'd expected—a little sour, and too warm, but fizzy and rich.

"Then there was the time," said someone else, "when Carol Dubois forgot her entrance in the Christmas play and Lucy Goodel and Jack Grange made up a whole scene."

"It was so good," Jed contributed, "no one knew the difference."

"And I stood there so fascinated and mixed up I didn't even know I'd missed my entrance," laughed a girl whom Melissa vaguely recognized as Carol Dubois.

It went on like that for nearly an hour—warm and friendly around the fire, faces glowing amber. The moon had gone behind a cloud so it was very dark beyond the flames, and the stars seemed to be fading; it was hot and still again—but perhaps that was also the heat from the fire. Hot as it was, though, Linnet stayed close to Melissa, right against her knee, touching her.

"Here," said Jed, handing her a bottle of beer. "I've got to go." He stood up and then looked down at her. "Melissa," he said softly, "Melissa, this is for you. I mean my part of it. Later, in the village, the Eights are supposed to leave the school to the Sevens. But I mean it for you, even though I guess you'll be back in Boston next year. I—I'm glad you came to Fours Crossing and I'll—well, I guess I'll miss you." Then he was gone, and Melissa, again without thinking, took a long swallow of the beer he'd handed her.

Linnet scrambled up, growling, and knocked the beer out of Melissa's hand.

"Wow!" someone shouted. "That's some watchdog!"

Everyone laughed, and Melissa, embarrassed, looked away.

It was then that her eye caught a small movement at the edge of the woods, beyond the flames. The slightest stirring of a leaf, as if it had been brushed against. A flash of white. A glint of gold.

One of the policemen, she tried to tell herself.

But Linnet looked in the same direction, and her hackles rose. Then, as one of the Eights started a song, she threw back her head and barked twice—quick, sharp barks, as if calling someone.

Any further sound was drowned out by the singing.

They went through all the songs they'd learned in school, and all they'd learned from the radio, and in church, and at home. Melissa joined in when she knew the words and the rest of the time just listened. As time went on and the fire burned lower, she felt lulled by the music, at peace with the summer's newness and the village—my village, she thought sleepily; it really is now, even if sometimes some of the people *are* rotten, like to Rhiannon—and I *won't* leave; or if I have to, I'll come back when I'm grown up, and I'll live here always . . .

A boy and a girl stood up, the girl in white, the boy in black, facing each other solemnly on opposite sides of the bonfire. The flames were low, and smoky. The two held out their hands to the smoke, as if bathing in it. Then they spread their arms, reaching for the hands of the people on either side of them. All the Eights stood, holding out their hands to the sweet-smelling smoke. Then, on a silent signal, they all turned, facing the Sevens, and with their hands wafted the smoke toward them.

"What's it for?" Melissa whispered to Tommy, fascinated.

"I don't know," said Tommy, his eyes on Jed. "Maybe no one does. I've never seen it, either. I guess each class learns from the one above, so it can be repeated each year."

Now each eighth-grader reached into the edge of the fire, where the embers had cooled, and pulled out a fragment or two of charred wood. Melissa saw Jed pull out two, and slowly circle the fire till he was standing before her and Tommy, holding out the wood.

"I give you oak," he said to them both; "guard it well. Speak nothing of it, or of what you have seen this night. A year from now, start your own fire with fresh kindling, but add this, to link your fire with ours, and with all others before it. And as you let the smoke cleanse you, know that you have served your apprenticeship here and that you are of Fours Crossing from that moment on, forever."

The murmur all around them, Melissa realized, was other Eights saying the same words to Sevens of their choosing, and she thought suddenly of the pride with which she had heard her own father and Joan's say, "I'm a Fours Crossing man."

But before she could take the thought further, or look at Tommy, Jed had thrust the charred bit of oak into her hand and joined the other Eights dancing around the fast-dying fire. It was an odd, devilish sight suddenly—the black silhouetted bodies leaping frenziedly around and sometimes over the glowing coals. Then she was pulled to her feet—not by Jed, by someone she barely knew—and Tommy was, and Joan, and all the other Sevens, and they were all dancing now, whirling around the fire as it died, sometimes singing, sometimes stooping to pick up and swallow from a partly full beer bottle, sometimes just whooping and laughing. The sound was joyous at first, as if in celebration. But slowly—perhaps it was the heat —it changed and became raucous, even cruel. Over it all, Linnet barked again as if calling, and this time there were distant answering barks.

And then, at the height of the frenzied dance, a tall figure lumbered out of the woods, holding what looked like a basket in his hand. One of the boys, apparently not seeing him, shouted, "It's time to get the sticks!" and each eighth-grader picked up a bundle of twigs from a pile near the fire and thrust it into the dying coals. Flames leaped up from twenty torches—twenty-one, as the oddly dressed stranger thrust his own larger bundle into the coals also. "Come," the stranger shouted, beckoning, "and purify at last!"

As his torch flared into flame, Melissa saw that the man was encased in wicker.

The procession of Sevens and Eights formed behind him as if he were part of it, had always been part of it. Maybe he is, Melissa tried to reassure herself; no one seems to think anything of his being here.

But just then her pendant grew so hot it almost burned her

chest, and Linnet pressed close to her, separating her from the group and growling—and Melissa saw the wicker man's face before he, laughing, put the basket-mask over his head.

He was the hermit.

20

He led them, running, down the mountain, their torches streaming flames into the night. Where are Chief Dupres's men, Melissa wondered frantically—but probably they're too far away to see, and of course no one is calling for them, so why should they think anything's wrong? It was clear that no one except Melissa had seen who the wicker man was, as if everyone was crazed with the night, or the beer, or his magic. Melissa tried to shout for the police—Linnet wouldn't let her leave the group—but her voice was lost in the cries of the others, and the police, of course, would be listening for her voice alone or for Jed's, and would probably ignore anything that sounded like part of the celebration.

And in the village, Melissa thought wildly as she ran, with Linnet urging her forward, they must be expecting to see people running with torches—no one's going to realize anything's wrong . . .

Melissa tried to run ahead to find Jed, to reason with him, to tell him something terrible was going to happen, but she couldn't catch up; it was as if the night and the dance and the drink had given everyone else uncanny strength; it was all she could do to stay close behind, with Linnet.

As they came down off Round Top, Melissa heard Linnet bark once more, and Ulfin, as if on guard, broke away from a spot near the river and ran past Jed and to her, touching noses with Linnet quickly and then nudging Melissa. She felt better with him there—until the hermit shouted, "Once around the green," and everyone followed, running.

Melissa could see people looking out of their windows and doors, and then one by one ducking hastily inside again; she could see from their faces that they did realize the procession was different this time, but that they didn't know in what way, or what to do.

"First your false school, children!" cried the hermit, and now Melissa caught glimpses of the faces of her classmates and of the Eights. The faces of most of her classmates wore looks of horror and many dropped back, but the Eights ran with glazed eyes as if their minds were empty. With great effort, urged on by the dogs, Melissa reached Jed at last and caught his arm—but the eyes he turned on her were as blind as those of his classmates; as if drugged, he moved away.

The hermit lifted his torch high in front of the school and waved it. "Your school is false," he cried to the Eights. "It denies your history, teaches only evil lies. Come, give not the false school to your younger friends, but give them instead the true gift of no school." He laughed—the hermit's old laugh, a high, thin cackle, shattering what little beauty remained in the night.

Something returned to Jed's eyes at the sound. He blinked, shook his head—and then over his face passed such a look of revulsion and horror that Melissa knew with relief he had returned to himself at last.

But there were others between them now and she couldn't reach him.

"Fire purifies!" the hermit was shouting; Melissa saw the door of the police station burst open. "That is the lesson you need learn from this night. I will teach you true things, not the falseness they teach here. I will be your teacher, your leader, your priest. Come, the torches. Then on to the cruel false church. And then—and then the witch. Come, the torches!"

"Oh, my God!" Melissa screamed, as the hermit began breaking windows with his burning torch and thrusting it flame first inside. At a distance Melissa saw the horror on Jed's face grow as both of them, still separated, helplessly watched the Eights begin imitating the hermit, first slowly, then more quickly. "No!" Jed shouted, shaking himself. Melissa saw him desperately trying to catch up to his classmates, but she could see that his feet were still leaden. "No! It's not like this—this is wrong!" he shouted. "Can't you see? It's wrong!"

But they paid no attention—elbowed both him and Melissa aside, nearly knocked Tommy down, left Joan far behind with the other equally shocked, frightened, and bewildered Sevens.

"Fire Department!" Tommy yelled then. "Quick!"

He raced across the green, where Melissa could see more men already assembling. Joan ran toward Chief Dupres, who was now halfway to the school, one hand on his gun and a look of dismay on his face. Two other policemen—the ones from Round Top, Melissa was sure—charged onto the green from the bridge road, looking equally bewildered. Melissa tried to follow Tommy, but Linnet wouldn't let her. "Linnet, no!" she shouted, trying to skirt her, but then she saw what the dog wanted, for the hermit had left the Eights and had turned toward the bridge. When Melissa followed, she saw him greeting as if by plan a group of dark shapes gathered there, some raising bottles to their lips, all lighting new torches from his huge one, laughing.

They were not Eights; they were not even Sevens or children at all, but men, with Mr. Titus at their head. In the brightening torchlight, Melissa recognized many of the same angry faces she'd seen around Mr. Titus at the meeting.

"The witch!" the hermit cried when these new torches had been lit—and the men turned toward the bridge and Round Top.

As Linnet urged her forward, Melissa saw Ulfin push against Jed roughly with his nose and then his whole body; finally, he took Jed's hand in his mouth and tugged; Melissa waited till Jed slowly began to move and then ran past him with Linnet after the hermit. She heard a splash as Jed and Ulfin crossed the bridge, but didn't dare turn to look.

Wildly, leaving chaos behind in the village, the handful of men who had followed the hermit raced up the mountain toward the remaining glow from the fire. Their torches blazed high; Melissa realized they would not need to replenish them before putting them to Rhiannon's house.

Or Rhiannon.

There was a loud curse ahead, and the men stopped so suddenly they piled into one another.

The moon broke away from the cloud that had been obscuring it and there suddenly in the path ahead, where the underbrush grew close on either side, was Dian, capering back and forth, up and down, blocking the way, butting the men back as they tried to pass, evading their thrust-out torches with ease, as if it were a game.

"Cursed goat!" cried one of the men. "Someone get it!"

But Dian wouldn't be gotten; she moved too quickly for the men, playing with them, teasing them—but Melissa knew her purpose was more.

As Dian danced, slowing the men momentarily, Jed and Ulfin, both of them dripping wet, caught up to Melissa. "Ulf shoved me into the river," Jed said sheepishly. "Dad used to say a good dunking sobers one up—Ulf must've heard. Melissa, there has to have been something in that beer. I had less than the others, luckily. But—well, it was weird. I hardly knew what was happening. You must have been right about—Holy cow!"

Flames from the bonfire ahead of them, suddenly rekindled, leaped up to the moonlit sky, higher than before, putting the men in awe. The faint sound of sirens came from the village below.

And the faint sound of harp music from above.

Mr. Titus, Melissa saw, rubbed his eyes.

"Where—what?" he said as the music grew louder.

"Forward!" cried the hermit, brandishing his dying torch; it had been burning longer than the others. "To the fire—see, it glows for us. To the witch!"

The men followed, but some of them grumbled now, as if confused. "Maybe he had them drink it, too," said Jed. "Something's wearing off for them, anyway. Look."

Two or three of the men had fallen behind and seemed to be discussing going back to the village. One of them looked toward Jed and Melissa; Melissa heard the words "crazy" and "kids here."

But the dogs urged Jed and Melissa on, and Dian pranced in front of the hermit, just out of reach, taunting him, leading him forward.

More men dropped back, avoiding Jed's and Melissa's eyes as they passed, and by the time Jed and Melissa got to the fire, it was just them, Mr. Titus, and the hermit.

And standing at the fire, her blue cloak billowing though there was no wind, was Rhiannon.

"The witch!" cried the hermit again to Mr. Titus, thrusting his now-cold torch into the soaring flames. "The witch!"

Rhiannon stood unmoving, expressionless, her harp now slung across her back. Over her shoulders, Melissa saw, she wore a blue-and-brown shawl—from the loom, Melissa thought irrelevantly; she must have finished it.

The hermit turned to speak to Mr. Titus, saw Jed and Melissa, and growled horribly. "You!" he snarled, his basket-mask falling off his face. "You will burn also! Traitors! Eben, Tabitha—Ulfin! It is your doing, all of it. You hold back the Ways still . . ."

A cry came from Mr. Titus's throat and he clutched his own face as if to tear away what his senses now told him was true. "My God!" he moaned, "my God. You're—you're Eli John Dunn, the hermit!" And he fled in panic down the mountain.

"It is you, Eli John," said Rhiannon, stepping forward, calm and splendid. "It is you who hold back the Ways. You hold back the good of the New and revive in your agony that which is bad of the Old. Wicker clothes are for criminals, not for priests, and in that you have chosen well, for criminal you have become. You are a disgrace to our band, to your own ancestors, who came long ago from many lands to live in peace and to worship in this lovely place. Our people wished to grow as this place grew. You would hold them back, even now."

She walked slowly toward the hermit as she spoke, but he remained motionless, so that soon he was standing with his back to the fire, Rhiannon on one side and Melissa behind her. Jed was next to Melissa, and the dogs flanked the hermit, with Dian near Linnet, her tail and ears twitching.

"You," growled the hermit, turning to Rhiannon, "you have no business in this place, come from far away as you did to destroy me."

"No, Eli John," said Rhiannon sadly. "Not to destroy you, but to save you. But, alas, you seem beyond saving." She held out her hand to him. "There is still time," she said softly. "You can still go back. They will not hurt you, the people of the court that tried you. They will try to heal, as I have tried. Who knows? Their new ways may succeed where my older ones have failed."

But the hermit ignored her outstretched hand, and Melissa remembered that Rhiannon had once said one could only heal a creature who wanted to be healed. She was about to try to plead with the hermit herself to take this last chance when he stepped toward her, his eyes gleaming and bitter. "It is you," he said, the words rasping and hissing, "you who poison my son, who sour the Ways—you with your sharp tongue, your mind that sees only forward . . ."

"I don't see only forward now," Melissa said, trying not to cower. "I—you and Rhiannon both, you've taught me not to. And—and my mother, I . . ."

He lunged, reaching for her.

"The pendant!" Rhiannon shouted. "Melissa, the pendant!"

But Melissa, moved despite her fear by a compassion that filled her eyes with tears, resisted, hands at her sides, twisting away.

Rhiannon seized her roughly and tore the pendant out of her blouse. For a moment it caught on Melissa's collar and she saw the dogs and Jed move toward her protectively and her mind, the fear returning, flashed gratitude. And then the hermit lunged once more and Melissa felt her own hand go

195

up and wrench her collar aside as Rhiannon freed the pendant and held it high. The moonlight played on the cross, the carved leaves, the cipher letters, the never-ending circular shape.

"Aaaaaaaaaiiiiiiiieeeeee!"

The hermit's shriek was terrible as he reeled back. The wicker flared as the flames rose to engulf it, and the hermit vanished.

For a moment there was no sound.

"It is over for now, my daughter," Rhiannon said gently.

21

Melissa and Jed stood as if turned to stone, staring into the empty fire. The dogs moved away, Ulfin more shakily than Linnet.

"Is he . . . ?" Melissa asked when she could speak. But she could not yet look at Rhiannon. The fire had died as quickly as it had flared, and there was now no trace of the wicker or of the hermit, though the woods stirred as if a great wind had passed.

"No," said Rhiannon gently, "no, he did not die as mortals die. The Old gave him that, though I was not sure the power could still be used. He has changed merely, gone elsewhere."

Melissa, only partly understanding, buried her head in Rhiannon's bosom. "I—I did it," she sobbed. "Rhiannon, I . . ."

"Hush, my daughter," Rhiannon said, stroking her hair. "You did not. You were the agent; for a moment you opened the door between." She tipped Melissa's chin up and gently wiped her eyes.

"I didn't know that was what it meant," Melissa said miserably. "If I had, I wouldn't—it's horrible, horrible . . ."

"He did not die," Rhiannon repeated emphatically. "Nor did he suffer. Because of you, child, the Old could be merciful. It was not always so." When Melissa still did not speak, she added, "It was I who held up the pendant—be comforted."

"That's right, you know," said Jed, touching Melissa's shoulder. "You didn't even push or anything. It *was* Rhiannon who held up that—that thing."

Melissa turned to him, her face wet with tears. "I *knew*," she said. "I knew he'd step back if he saw it. And—and I helped free it."

"I bet you didn't even think," said Jed. Then fiercely he said, "Melissa, didn't you hear Rhiannon? She said it was merciful, because of you." He put his hand more firmly on Melissa's shoulder. "She's trying to tell you it wasn't like burning witches, even if that's what the hermit would have done."

Rhiannon very gently pushed Melissa away from herself and toward Jed, until he was holding her awkwardly. "Oh, look," he said, desperation in his voice, "he'd have grabbed you, Melissa."

Melissa realized that Rhiannon had moved away; she wrenched free of Jed. But Rhiannon held up her hand. "I must go," she said quietly. "I am finished here. No—no, my children, do not try to follow me."

"Rhiannon," said Jed, as she began to move away, "wait. Wait. Is—is it over? Is Fours Crossing safe?"

Rhiannon smiled faintly. "It is never over," she told them. "But the door has begun to open now for the joining." She took the blue-and-brown shawl from her shoulders and settled it firmly over Melissa's, smiling. And then she backed away from them in the darkness. Two small shapes went with her— Linnet and Dian.

And Ulfin, trembling, howled wolflike with the loss.

Bits and pieces remained; Melissa walked through them in a daze. First, the drought broke that night, and the next day was beautiful, so the graduation reception was held outdoors under clear, cool skies, with everyone remarking on how lucky it was that the school building had escaped serious fire damage. At graduation itself, Gran looked every bit as proud as Seth when Jed accepted his diploma. Mr. Henry Ellison spoke, reminding everyone that it was Midsummer, when the sun reaches its peak and then starts its long but steady descent into winter. "As you leave us," he said to the Eights, "remember to turn as the sun turns on this day, and come back to us here in Fours Crossing from wherever else you may go throughout your lives." That made Melissa think of her father, who had arrived just in time for the ceremony and slid into the seat next to her, after a whispered conversation with Gran, saying, "I don't think I dare leave again for a long time, pigeon. Thank goodness, you're all right!"

"Congratulations," Melissa said to Jed at the reception, through her daze and the thickness in her throat.

"Oh, don't be so glum," her father said, hugging her. "He'll see you graduate next year."

She and Jed both stared at him.

He grinned, and Gran chuckled. "Mr. Henry Ellison's offered me the job of Forest Keeper," he said, "since there's no other adult Dunn left now who can take it. And the hospital up in Hiltonville could use a fund-raiser on their staff."

"Whoopee!" shouted Tommy, who'd been standing nearby with Joan. "That's one good thing today, anyway."

Then there was the official inquiry to get through, an investigation into the hermit's supposed disappearance. It would have been easy, since there had been no witnesses except Jed, Melissa, and Rhiannon—and maybe even safer—to let it remain as the other Eli's disappearance had remained back in

1725, with no one saying anything about what had really happened. But as Jed said, besides being untrue, that might lead to the hermit's somehow coming back again. Melissa agreed, thinking but not saying that hiding what had happened might also close the door that Rhiannon said had begun to open. So she and Jed told the court that they had been there, and that Rhiannon had also, but that she had gone into the woods afterward. They described as closely as they could what had happened, and left it to the court to puzzle out why no trace of the hermit remained when the fire had grown cold. When Melissa was asked, "Why did you and Rhiannon hold up your necklace?" she said honestly, "We'd seen him move away from it before. I guess it was the only thing we could think of doing so he wouldn't grab me." To "Why didn't you run?" she said truthfully, "There wasn't time; he was right there—at me."

And so, after long deliberation, the court tentatively ruled that the hermit had once more escaped. He was again listed as "wanted" by the police, and bulletins went out to many states and to Canada. But slowly, as time went on and he did not return and was not heard from, the village's fear subsided.

After supper on the day of the ruling, Melissa, Jed, and Ulfin went up to Round Top once more. There was a charred spot where the police had scraped up the fire's ashes, but lying beside it were four fresh and leafy branches—rowan, as on the summer plate, and maple, hemlock, and oak.

"Maybe she's still here after all," said Jed, fingering the rowan leaves.

But Melissa knew even before they got to Rhiannon's cottage that she wouldn't be.

The clearing was silent and empty, with only the brook for music. It seemed a sad and lonely place now, with Rhiannon gone, and Linnet and Dian. "As if they were never here," said Melissa, peering into the cottage window, half hoping to see the blue and brown of the shawl still on the loom instead of back at Gran's in her bureau drawer, where it now lay; hoping to see the kettle on the fire, the kittens playing on the hearth.

But inside, the cottage was dark and cobwebby, the loom empty, and the fire cold.

Jed called her to the back, where the cages were. "Not quite everyone's gone," he said softly, standing before one cage whose door, like the doors of the others, was open.

The other cages were empty, but in this one the young sparrow hawk stood perched on a branch as if waiting for them, even though his wing was now healed. He cocked his head, fixing them with his bright eyes.

"One of us had better take him home," said Jed. "Looks as if he doesn't want to be wild."

"Yes," said Melissa. She held out her arm, remembering how Rhiannon had handled him, and the sparrow hawk hopped onto her wrist, flapped his wings once, and settled as if he belonged there.

"I wonder," said Jed, watching, "if it's quite over yet."

With her free hand, as a cool wind sighed across Round Top, Melissa unconsciously touched the chain of her pendant.

"I wonder, too," she said.

Author's Note

Midsummer, which occurs around the time of the summer solstice, has for centuries been linked with the Christian feast of St. John's Eve and Day—June 23–24. However, customs in Fours Crossing and those celebrated by the hermit and Rhiannon stem more directly from pagan than from Christian traditions. Hence the relationship of Midsummer here with the actual date of the solstice.

Nancy Garden
Carlisle, Massachusetts